What People Are Saying About

SILVER TO GOLD

I have known Jen for over ten years and I have watched her live the Silver to Gold adventure. I have witnessed the birth of this book as she talked and wrote this epic story. It came out of her soul not just her mind. This adventure will stir, invigorate, and compel you to go for the Gold. I highly recommend it.

Robert Fulton, Vineyard International Coordinator Emeritus

An incredible account of a girl who refused to let go of her dreams. This book is so encouraging, a must read for those who get weighed down by other people refusing to join them on their journey. Keep dreaming and keep walking!

Leanne Taylor, 20, student, UK

This is a modern-day *Pilgrim's Progress*, a tale that resonates with both science fiction and allegory of a young woman who rejects a life of compromise and finds her true fulfillment in overcoming obstacles and discouragements to reach her higher goals. This is inspirational reading that will resonate with any of us who have been tempted to give up. Once you pick up this fascinating story you will not want to put it down.

Dr. Allan Anderson, author of *Spreading Fires*

Silver to Gold is a story of extraordinary courage. The heroin's determination not to settle for anything less than the total fulfillment of her dreams inspires us not to accept mediocrity. We all have dreams hidden in our hearts, but for some reason we hold back and are scared to pursue them, or we give up along the way. This is a message of hope, showing that it really is possible to achieve our greatest goals.

After reading this story I was inspired to take my dream of writing more seriously.

Alice Claire Stapleton, 20, UK

Silver to Gold is about dreams; recognizing them, being inspired by them, pursuing them, and turning them into reality. This is a challenging and provocative book which asks perceptive questions for a multicultural society grappling with the economic and social fall out of a global recession. I will be recommending it as a "must read" in my personal and working life.

Andrew Pain, Accredited Life and Business Coach at Impact Life Ltd

Silver to Gold is an inspirational story to dream seemingly impossible dreams. It is an encouragement to press through every challenge and obstacle, until our vision becomes a reality. Jen is an awesome young revolutionary who has courageously pressed in to the dreams of God for her own life regardless of the cost, and counted it all as joy! I highly recommend this book to everyone who is not prepared to settle for anything less than the very best!

Heidi Baker, Ph.D, Founding Director, Iris Ministries, Inc.

Silver to Gold

Lisa,
You rock! May you
be inspired beyond your
wildest dreams and thrive
in your true destiny to the
fullest. All the best my
friend! — Jennifer C-Mateer

Note to the reader:
*There is a song printed on page 78 that is more powerful heard than read. If at all possible, set it up beforehand in order to listen to it in the story without breaking the flow. It can be found by going on iTunes by searching for the original 1999 version of the song entitled "Goodbye" by the band Plankeye, written by Eric Balmer and Luis Garcia. Lyrics reprinted by permission from EMI. Copyright © 1999 Stonewall Tozer Pub. (SESAC) We Own Your Songs, Inc. (SESAC) (adm. by EMI CMG Publishing) International copyright secured. All rights reserved. Used by permission

Cover image by Chris Lauer, headshot by Joanna Hield Photography, and cover design by IE Design.

Published by Silver to Gold
www.silvertogold.com

ISBN: 0-9842370-0-3
ISBN-13: 9780984237005

Printed in the United States of America and the United Kingdom

Silver to Gold

A Journey of Young Revolutionaries

Jennifer A. Miskov

This book is dedicated to those who have stepped into the infinite abyss of uncertainty to follow their hearts.

Prison

Will I ever break free
From this mold, it's binding me
Hard as stone, the cast that's enclosing me
I want to move but I can't break loose

Crack this prison
Soften the clay that surrounds me
I want to dance, to run, to play
Will I crawl in the dirt forever?
How I long to fly
To feel the air with surrendered wings
To glide in the warmth of your sunshine
Show me the way...

-J.M.

Intersection

This is a mistake.

The moment she saw the first of the bearded men, her hope turned to despair. At nineteen, Desire felt she was too young to die.

The king's horsemen were now upon her and the others, forcing them to an abrupt halt just outside the Bronze Hills. Desire frantically scanned the wasteland, desperately searching for a way to make it to the mountains. When she peered through the diminishing darkness, she saw thousands of foot soldiers advancing from behind.

Her heart beat accelerated.

Joshua stood nearby. Even he couldn't save her now.

She thought of her father. He would be devastated when he found out she hadn't made it.

While the vile men on horseback waited for the rest of their comrades, they began to taunt Desire and the others.

Two of the heavily decorated soldiers galloped their horses directly toward her. She stood in front of Dawn to protect her from the oncoming impact. Just seconds before crushing them underfoot, the men pulled back their horses, and then lined up to do it all over again. Desire despised these soldiers who toyed with her and the others, treating them like prey.

As the marching men came closer to the group of seventy, one of the soldiers yelled in their direction, "Prepare for battle, you scum!" He held up his shield, quivering in jest.

Desire's heart sank even deeper when she heard them burst into laughter. She looked to Joshua for help.

Joshua, only a few years older than Desire, showed no visible signs of being afraid; he only seemed to grow in stature. He met her trepidation with composure. She felt his eyes convey the message: *It's going to be alright.*

But how was it going to be alright? She saw no way out of their hopeless situation. Yet when she saw Joshua turn toward the advancing army, she could read the determination on his face as his green eyes focused intently. She had no trouble interpreting his look.

It was time to take action.

He raised his arm and then slammed it down, signaling the others to beat their drums. He sang his hope with authority, "We will overcome! Yes, we will overcome..."

She saw Dawn and the other Young Revolutionaries soon echo his call.

Singing "we will overcome" when they were completely surrounded by thousands of the king's soldiers was ludicrous to Desire. She thought Joshua had gone mad. She saw no hint of hope, no point in singing a song like that, especially at that moment.

Nevertheless, she decided to join in, hesitantly, trying to convince herself the possibility of escape existed. Even near death, she attempted to stay true to the name given to her according to her mother's last request, to follow her *desire* for a free and full life. She would not only do it for herself, but she would do it for her mother, too. In the open field just outside the place she wanted to escape, her hope melted away with each approaching step of the army.

She desperately wished she had stayed back. She had already learned to deal with the misery and injustice of the Bronze Hills once before. *Alive and oppressed is better than dead and free*, she thought. But there was no going back now, and she knew she would receive no mercy from her enemies.

The horsemen were in front of her, and the foot soldiers were moving in on them from behind.

Twenty-five feet...

Desire's body started to shake. She saw Dawn trembling too.

Twenty feet...

She heard the soldiers' mocking. "Where you gonna run to now?"

"Thought we would just let you go, huh?"

Desire's singing muffled to a stop when she heard the soldiers' taunts. The other Young Revolutionaries were intimidated into a silence as well. The soldiers carried on jeering at them, "Never learn your lesson, do ya?"

"You should know by now, there's no escaping King Laird."

Desire cringed when she heard the soldier say his name. She hated that name more than any other, for it belonged to the man who had reduced her father to a mere slave and who allowed her uncle to be murdered. King Laird destroyed families and his burden was heavy. Hearing his name only served to renew Desire's fear and shatter her remaining hope for leaving his kingdom.

Fifteen feet...Scanning the looming mass of armed men, Desire's gaze stuck on one of the soldiers. Suddenly, she realized she recognized him. He noticed her too. She watched his mouth twist into a cruel smirk.

Then, looking from her worn sandals, to the jagged edges of her ripped trousers, to her white blouse, he said with a nasty grin, "I hope we get some time together."

She felt herself shrink in that instant. She wished she could be crushed into the dark dust that made up that isolated plain *before* he made it to her.

Ten feet...Desire could see the whites of his eyes as he came straight for her.

Five feet...She backed up and was pushed against her friends. Dawn was there. Desire found her hand and squeezed tight, sure it would be the last time they would see each other.

The filthy soldier seized Desire's arm. She could instantly feel his fingerprints stamped into her body where his hand gripped. She was forced to let go of Dawn's hand.

She saw Joshua captured next. They punched him in the face and then spat on him, cursing him for trying to lead the group away. Soldiers held his arms while several others guarded him. Desire noticed the resilience in his eyes as he looked at her. She wanted them to stop beating him, but there was nothing she could do. Dawn was taken next, then all the others.

Desire didn't fight back. She and the others were outnumbered a hundred to one.

As the soldier pulled her back toward the Bronze Hills, all of a sudden, a strong gust of wind from the west violently swept through the battlefield. Desire's brown hair flew over her face. She brushed it away with her free hand.

Thunder boomed from the east.

The earth vibrated and the air whirled the dust all around them.

She heard strong melodies hovering in the air beyond the front lines.

While the rising sun came from the east, ominous clouds came from the north and filled the battlefield with a mysterious silver lining.

What was this new and overpowering noise?

She looked up at the brute clinging to her and saw his eyes tighten. He swung her with him as he turned in circles, looking every which way.

When he shifted Desire back towards the east, she saw the silhouette of an immense army approaching. She had never seen people pass through the isolated hills before. She had no idea who the mysterious army was or where it had come from, but it was marching straight towards King Laird's soldiers. Uncertain hope welled up inside of her. Maybe she would make it out alive after all.

Chaos filled the dusty scene.

The disgusting man who towered over her small frame finally released his hold.

Rubbing the skin where bruises were soon to appear, she stepped back and looked around, her mouth wide open. She saw the men release Joshua. He fell to the ground but then slowly rose back to his feet.

Every face she saw was etched in fear and awe.

She watched the disoriented men stumble over each other and fall out of rank.

"Realign! Realign!" a commander screamed.

"Leave them! Move, move! Get in formation!" another soldier yelled.

They shuffled around, slamming into and knocking each other over.

"Get up! Take your weapons!" One of the horsemen shouted.

Desire saw the soldiers struggle to regroup. They were forced to abandon her and the other Young Revolutionaries.

"This way," Joshua shouted in the midst of the commotion as he waved his arm toward the west and away from the frantic scene. "Let's go, let's go. Hurry up!"

For Desire, everything moved in slow motion. She just stood there, astounded by the divine sign. Joshua grabbed her arm and pulled her in the direction of the others. "Come on, this is our chance."

Without looking back, Desire ran with Joshua, Dawn, and the others towards the Silver Mountains. Carrying her small pack, she ran like she never had before. Her lungs burned and her heart pounded.

When the group was far enough away from the battlefield and it was clear they were not being pursued, Joshua turned to look behind him. Desire followed his lead, then Dawn and the others looked in the same direction.

Desire's adrenaline was still pumping, and her curiosity increased as she saw the multitude of soldiers fight against each other in the distance.

"That was *so* close!" she said while shaking her head.

Dawn didn't say a word. Desire thought she must still be in shock.

"Amazin', just amazin'," Victoria, the young woman standing near them, piped in. "Hey, you're still shakin'."

"I know. I can't calm down. I can't believe we made it!" Desire responded. "Where did they come from?" She asked, gasping between breaths.

"I have *no* idea," Dawn answered.

"Don't know either, just glad we're out of there," Victoria said.

"Incredible!" Desire said, overwhelmed by the growing euphoria.

Bemused over the other army, it also struck Desire that she was now moving farther away from her father. She prayed that the strange army would overthrow King Laird's kingdom and lift off the heavy burden placed upon the people. She couldn't be sure, though, if they might do just the opposite.

Grieving that she might never know the outcome of the battle or its implications, she continued to hurry along with the others towards the Silver Mountains.

Part One

Free At Last

Well into nightfall, they set up camp in the open terrain to rest for a few hours. Joshua and a few others stood guard throughout the night in case the soldiers came after them. As the sky lightened early the next morning, they quickly packed up their things and continued towards the mountains.

Desire and the others finally arrived late that night at the base of the first mountain.

The whole group bustled with excitement as they set up camp. Since there was no sign that the soldiers were following them, they made a fire at the foot of what was known in the Legend as Freedom Mountain.

Pure celebration filled the late night. Joshua started a rhythm on their only remaining drum while Desire and the others danced victoriously around the flames. Desire saw Dawn break into a celebration dance for the first time.

As the festivities died down, Desire took in her surroundings with her friend Sam sitting next to her.

"I've never seen the stars sparkle so brightly," her eyes twinkled at their sight.

"They look so different from here," Sam said while brushing his blonde hair away from his forehead. "I already feel lighter here, like a big weight's been lifted off my back," he continued.

"Me too. There's something so much better about this place than the Bronze Hills. I can feel it," Desire said.

"You're right, I can feel it too. And did you notice the silver on the mountain top?"

"Yeah, I've never seen anything like it before."

"Me neither," Sam said with a smile.

"I still can't believe we're *free*," Desire said.

Desire had always felt supported by her friendship with Sam which had started a few years back. They were close in age and Desire used to pass his home after her long days at work. Sam's father oversaw work projects for the king, a job which came with some benefits. His father got first pick of the king's leftovers and whatever else was left behind by the soldiers. While Sam, a slightly stout yet built young man, had more privileges because of this, he always struggled to enjoy the king's delicacies because he knew exactly where they came from.

King Laird was never meant to be king in the first place. He only seized power after stabbing his reformist brother in the back the day after their father's death. Those who spoke against him were kidnapped by his secret group of informers and then publically hung. He left their bodies outside the courtyard as a reminder to the living never to challenge his tyranny. His burden was heavy; despair, hopelessness, and even suicide were common among those who lived under his rule. His piercing dark eyes suited him well and revealed the pure evil of his soul.

Desire turned towards Sam. "Ever since I was little I always wondered if I would make it out of that kingdom, if

I would ever be able to break out from under King Laird's control...and now we're here."

She remembered the story her father told her about a man who followed the Legend but wasn't as lucky. "He tried to rally some of the people to escape with him but no one was daring enough. So one day he decided to try and escape on his own."

Sam listened closely as she continued. "He made it all the way to the foothills of the Silver Mountains. He came close enough to see the silver gray granite on this mountaintop just before he was captured. He was brought to the king's courtyard, beaten, tortured, and then hung in broad daylight. He became another victim of the king's evil intimidation tactics."

"That's horrible," Sam said.

"My dad told me that in this man's last breath, he prayed that the Legend of the Pastures would stir the hearts of the next generation."

"Well, I guess he'd be happy if he could see us now." With his arms folded across his chest, Sam let out a deep breath and smiled.

"I later found out that this man was a close friend of my dad's," Desire said and then looked down. "I think that after losing his friend like this, then losing my mom, it must have crushed any spark, any hope in him of following the Legend." Her eyes examined the intricate crevices in the ground. Silence settled. Her father was absent from her life now.

"I just wish he could be here now, see this place, feel this freedom." Desire wondered if she could have been more persuasive to get her father to come.

"I know what you mean." Sam put his arm around her. She leaned into him. He held her for a few moments before she got up and wished him good night.

While walking toward her tent, Desire felt secure when she caught a glimpse of Joshua standing guard.

The Flame

Desire was always so intrigued by him.
Joshua.

It made sense for his name to stand alone, to pause before describing him. He was someone she had always admired. *Well, who wouldn't?* Joshua was forced into the brick-making business at the age of thirteen because he was the only one who could provide for his family. He also helped his mother take care of things in the home. Desire never heard him complain about it either. After his father died, his mother fell into a deep depression. Because of his mother's fragile state, Joshua's younger sister Kaden became a huge problem. She ran around recklessly, causing trouble and rebelling against those who loved her. Joshua was the only one who was able to administer any sort of discipline for his sister.

Desire wondered what must be going on in his head. Was he as excited as the others about being there at the foot of Freedom Mountain? Or was he so intent on reaching the Pastures that, as far as he was concerned, the Silver Mountains were mere stepping stones to get there? It was so hard to tell with Joshua because he always wore a calm and steady expression on his face.

When Desire arrived at her makeshift tent, she entered to find Dawn and Kaden sleeping restlessly. Euphoric and energized by her newfound freedom, Desire also struggled to fall asleep that night. As she lay there, she remembered the moment she first heard about the journey several months before.

***

"I have to tell you something," Joshua said to Desire when he found her at her home. This was the first time she had seen him since he moved to the other side of the Bronze Hills years before.

"The stories of the Golden Pastures have haunted me lately," he said.

Desire knew the story well, as did everyone in the Bronze Hills. Originating with the Kane brothers, the Legend of the Golden Pastures had secretly been passed on through oral tradition for several hundred years. How much of this story was fact or fantasy wasn't clear. Desire knew that legends had a way of building into folklore over time.

Joshua told her about his three consecutive dreams concerning the Pastures.

"I woke up after each with a strong sense of peace and anticipation," he said.

She tried to grasp what that would feel like.

His enthusiasm increased as he continued, "I saw water, but not in a well. It was moving and then fell from a great height, higher than any of the hills around here. I saw colorful plants and new kinds of vegetation covering the land." He used the language found in the Legend to match what he had seen in his vivid dreams.

Desire struggled to make sense of the things he spoke of. She had never seen such things before.

"There's something special about that place. We *have* to go there," he said. "I feel it so powerfully; I feel like we're made for it."

A surge of excitement swept through her entire being when she heard his words.

Joshua looked into her blue eyes with deepening emotion, "It's time to break out of this place and follow the Legend. How much longer can we work for the king's soldiers? We don't have to be subjected to their abuse any longer."

He was right. Desire hated the way the soldiers looked at her when she brought them water as part of her daily tasks, how they brutally took advantage of Dawn one terrible night. She hated how King Laird encouraged his soldiers to be cruel to her people. Desire wanted to get as far away from him as she could. But it wasn't just freedom from his oppressive hold she was excited about, there was something more.

Joshua told her that he was destined to discover the new land. He said he was meant to be there, that something was pulling him towards it. It wasn't just for him. The others needed to be there, too.

He said he was ready to assemble the others, to call them to find life in the Golden Pastures, the place where he believed they would fully thrive. He felt the timing was right and believed the plan would resonate with the others as well. He hoped he could describe it well enough to convince them.

Desire felt her heart burn within her as he spoke of these things. Joshua was tapping into a dream she had in her own heart. Deep down, she always felt there was more to life. She hungered to be free and fully alive in every way, but she felt inhibited by the dark hills that constantly surrounded her, oppressing her with their shadows. She had spent so much time in the past gazing at the mountains in the distance, wondering what life outside the Bronze Hills would be like. Even beyond freedom from the Bronze Hills, she felt she was destined for something greater.

Her father used to speak of her mother's obsession with the Legend. Because of this, from childhood on, Desire was gripped by the promise of a full life in the Pastures. She felt that if she failed to stay true to her heart, she would be miserable; not just because she would be stuck in the Bronze Hills, but more so because she would be repressing who she was meant to be. She couldn't explain the pull Joshua spoke of, but she felt it too, an intense feeling inside drawing her towards more.

***

Desire could hardly believe that what they talked about months before was actually happening. As she lay on the hard ground in her makeshift shelter, she finally calmed down enough to rest a little. She had no idea what the next day would hold, but she couldn't wait for it to come.

Anticipation

Desire awoke to the sound of birds singing in the distance. Their sweet melodies tickled her ears and made her feel even more alive and expectant for the new day. She cleared the sleep from her eyes and stared at the blanket canopy above her, the roof of her new home until she reached the Pastures.

Her lips parted to release the smile growing inside her. She wasn't merely dreaming. It was true after all. It really was one of her first days of freedom. She turned to her left and saw Kaden still fast asleep, her brown hair flopped over the side of her face. When she looked on her other side, there was an empty space where Dawn had been. Desire poked her head out of the tent and saw Dawn standing nearby, gazing at the steadfast mountain before them.

Desire had met Dawn a few years before when they were paired together to scrub the floors in the king's courtyard. The two were also responsible for fetching well water for the filthy soldiers, a task Desire hated more than anything. Enduring much ridicule and mistreatment from the soldiers, the two became faithful confidantes.

Desire crawled out of the tent to join her.

"Morning."

Dawn, who was just a few years younger than Desire, returned her greeting with a smile then turned back to continue looking at the mountain that stood before them.

"Today's going to be a great day, I can feel it already," Desire stretched her arms to the sky, inviting the new free air to surge through her mind, body, and soul.

"We're free, we're actually free," responded Dawn.

"It's really happening. Can you believe it?" Desire said.

"I know, and I slept through the whole night. I haven't done that in so long."

Desire remembered the story Dawn told her of when the soldiers stormed into her home in the middle of the night and falsely accused her father of conspiracy against the king. She was forced to watch them beat him nearly to death. While her father lay almost unconscious on the floor, the soldiers took advantage of her mother right in front of her. They came for her next. Dawn regularly had nightmares ever since.

"Really, you slept well?" Desire asked in a hopeful tone.

Dawn nodded, her long black hair falling in front of her face. She tucked it behind her ear and said, "There's this release here that I've never felt before. I'm so glad to be away from the soldiers."

"Yeah, me too," Desire said.

"I feel such freedom here. This new life's going to be great," Dawn said as she pulled her arms to her chest.

"Yeah, it's going to be so much better than what we had before," Desire added, looking at the small clump of trees and the few scattered berry bushes at the base of the mountain.

"Can anything else compare with this?" Dawn said under her breath as she moved towards their tent.

"What did you say?" Desire asked.

"Oh, nothing." Dawn's slender body bent down as she leaned into the tent to wake Kaden.

After they packed up their blankets, Desire and her companions joined the others already assembled. Joshua saw them coming. "You ready for the hike?" he asked.

Dawn looked down while Kaden shouted, "Let's do it!"

Desire shared her grin with Joshua as she swung her pack over her shoulder. Her bag was filled with a rolled-up blanket and her only other change of clothes. Dawn carried some of the bread and another blanket, while Joshua and Sam brought the rope and water packs.

As Desire approached the side of the mountain, she felt taller, as if she had grown a few inches overnight. Joshua led the group up the mountain with Kaden and Victoria not far behind him. Desire thought Kaden would have sprinted and passed him by if she knew where she was going. Desire hiked with Dawn so that she could keep her safe. Desire's thin sandals didn't provide the best support but at least they protected the bottom of her feet from the thorns and rocks. Sam traveled behind them, staying near Desire most of the time.

As they continued to hike, Desire lost sight of the path the others had taken. Suddenly, it occurred to her that the stronger hikers ahead of them had completely disappeared up the mountainside. She and the other stragglers found themselves uncertain of where to go next. Desire examined the ground, looking for even a hint of the path the others had taken. She noticed a tiny trail of trampled bushes and weeds and decided that must have been the path they had taken.

She and the others followed the rough path and made it about midway up the mountain before she saw a large granite rock that blocked their route. Desire looked up and then scanned the area for another possible path. She found no other way around this boulder.

"We *have* to climb over," Sam announced.

Dawn's eyes widened as she looked to Desire.

"It won't be that bad, you'll see. Here, I'll go first," Desire said.

"I can give you a boost," Sam said as he naturally held out his hand to Desire.

He lifted Desire to where she could grip a small notch on the side of the rock. Steadily, she managed to bring her other hand over the top of the boulder to a small indentation and slide herself onto the top of the rock. Standing up, she swayed back and forth before finding her center.

"It looks safer to climb over here," Desire said, wiping the fresh scratches on her arm. She walked to her left and pointed it out to them below.

Desire saw panic on Dawn's face.

"It's not as bad as it looks, you can make it," Desire said while looking down at her.

Sam lifted Dawn up on the right side of the rock so that she could wedge her hand into a crevice in the rock. Dawn then found a foothold for both her feet. She bent her legs and prepared to leverage herself up when...

Dislocation

Putting weight on her right foot, Dawn pushed up. Her foot twisted off the small ledge. Suddenly, she screamed in pain.

With an expression as calm and controlled as she could manage, Desire called out, "Take hold of my hand."

Having already secured herself by wrapping her other hand around a tree, Desire reached out and clutched Dawn's hand.

Dawn continued to cling to the notch in the rock with one hand and squeezed Desire's hand with the other. Sam had both hands lifted high in case Dawn fell.

"Move your foot to the right, there's a ledge there," Sam said.

Desire could feel Dawn's grip weakening as she watched her scramble to find a foothold. Dawn finally found a place to put her foot down. She put all of her weight on her right foot and then pushed up. With that added momentum, Desire pulled her towards the top of the rock. Dawn swung her leg and slid over to where it was flat. She rolled over, closer to the mountain and away from the rock's edge.

"Let's sit you over here," Desire bent down and helped move her to a safer location.

"Ahhhhh!" Dawn yelled as she reached down and grabbed her left ankle.

Desire looked blankly at her. Uncomfortable dealing with pain, she just sat beside her.

Sam scurried up the rock. When he made it to the top, he sat near Dawn and examined her ankle.

He set his hand on her shoulder to calm her down. A few minutes later he moved a rock over and put his pack on top of it as a cushion to help elevate her leg.

After some time, Dawn was able to relax.

With her face still flushed and streaked with the remains of tears, Dawn looked at Desire.

"What can I do?" Desire said, jumping at any opportunity to help.

"Could you find me a stick...a walking stick or something?"

Wanting to do everything possible to alleviate Dawn's pain, Desire immediately went out looking for the perfect walking stick.

"I knew this was a bad idea," Desire overheard Dawn say to Sam.

Desire looked back and saw Sam give a half-grin to acknowledge Dawn. He put his arm under her leg to help steady her elevated foot.

"I found one," Desire yelled, feeling proud and awkward at the same time. She hurried back to join them.

They spent some time on the rock's ledge, resting and eating some of the bread they had brought. This downtime made Desire realize how annoyed she was that all the others had abandoned them up the mountain. She wondered if this accident might have been avoided if Joshua and Kaden had stayed back. She didn't say anything about her frustrations, it wouldn't help now.

They took some of the spare cloth used as tethers for the tent to wrap up Dawn's foot. Desire's wounded friend gathered her strength and said she was ready to move forward.

"You sure?" Desire asked.

"I'm fine, I'll be fine," Dawn replied.

"We can wait a little longer if you need the time."

"Let's just go now," Dawn said.

"Let me help you then." Sam supported her to stand, moving her arm around his shoulder. She grimaced with the first several steps.

Desire and Sam stayed with Dawn and took their time up the mountain, but their pace was greatly slowed. Desire thought that if they made it to the mountain's peak before sunset they would be okay. If not, she wondered whether they would have to climb in the dark, or sleep on the side of the mountain.

Desire noticed the stains on the underarms of Sam's shirt grow bigger as he helped Dawn struggle up the mountain. As they neared the top, the route narrowed and became steeper. There was only enough room to hike single file. Desire went first while Sam stayed behind Dawn. She limped up, using her walking stick for support.

They were the last ones to make it up the mountain that day. The cool air was refreshing after the hard climb. Joshua noticed the last arrivals and came to meet them. He looked at Dawn's foot and wrapped a cool cloth around it to reduce the swelling.

Joshua pointed out to the girls where Kaden had already set up their tent. Exhausted from the hike, they headed straight there. Standing outside and absorbing the view, Dawn leaned over to Desire and spoke in a quiet voice so as not to awaken Kaden.

"That hike wore me out," she said.

"It was a tough one, wasn't it?" Desire responded.

Dawn lifted her eyes to meet the horizon.

"The view from up here is beautiful, and a bit overwhelming," Dawn said, while gazing at the valley below that separated them from the chain of Silver Mountains ahead of them. Her fingers nervously tapped her walking stick without any set rhythm.

"Keep looking past the valleys and beyond the mountains. The Golden Pastures are out there somewhere, I just know it," Desire encouraged.

"But look at that isolated valley and those mountains. They must be even steeper than the one we just climbed. I don't know," Dawn said.

"A good night's sleep should help. You'll be okay. Your ankle will heal up in no time," Desire said as she examined the long valley and the mountain chain to the west.

They entered the tent and got situated. A small blanket and her pack for a pillow was about all Desire had to make it more like home.

As Desire lay there, fear, excitement, and wonder filled her mind in the silence. The silence was unlike any other she had experienced in her life, for it was a silence of freedom, of perspective, of new hope on the horizon, of wonder if she could actually make it to the Golden Pastures that lay ahead. She tossed and turned again before she finally wore herself out mentally and fell into an uneasy and dreamless sleep.

"Desire, you awake?" Dawn whispered the following morning while poking her friend's side. Desire had no choice but to wake up.

"Hey, can we talk?" Dawn asked.

Unlike Desire, Dawn was definitely a morning person. She was already wide-eyed and must have been waiting for Desire's first stirrings.

"I don't think I can do this."

"What?" Desire said, still groggy, wiping the sleep from her eyes as she pulled back the tattered blanket and sat up. "What are you talking about?"

Twist and Turn Away

"Freedom's all I ever wanted, and we have that now. That valley looks scary, and did you see all those mountains?" Dawn said.

"You'll be okay, we'll make it," Desire responded.

"But we can't even see the Pastures from here. Do we know for sure they exist?"

"Didn't you see all that just happened to us back there? You just have to believe. Everything will work out. It will be *so* worth it, you'll see," Desire said, clearing her throat.

"Hey, what's going on?" Kaden mumbled sleepily.

"I don't know. I'm fine here, really. This place is so much better than our old home," Dawn said.

Desire saw the look in Dawn's eyes. *Was she really serious about this nonsense?* "But we've only just started our journey," she said to her.

"What's happening?" Kaden asked again.

"I can make a home for myself with the others just down this mountain," Dawn continued.

"What others? Who are you talking about? What's going on?" Kaden asked while looking back and forth at Desire and Dawn.

Then, looking Dawn square in the eyes, Desire said, "You can't be talking about living *here?*"

Kaden chipped in, "Is that true? Will someone *please* tell me what's going on?"

"Okay, okay. Well, early this morning I heard people talking, so I went over to find out what was going on." Looking at Kaden, Dawn explained, "They want to settle at the foot of this mountain. I'm already injured anyway."

"What?" Kaden asked.

"But there's more for you," Desire attempted to re-envision her friend.

"Part of me wants to believe it's true...but you're asking me to endure deep valleys and climb high mountains in hope of a land I'm not even sure really exists."

"But it is true, it does exist. You'll see," Desire said with confidence.

"Maybe it does...maybe you're right. But I just don't think I can make it. The journey is going to be too hard. I'm not strong enough and I'll slow you all down. I'll never make it. I'll be fine here, really." Dawn got up to leave the tent. "Desire, you don't need to worry about me anymore. Thank you for everything," she said as she left. Desire stuck her head out of the tent and saw her limp towards a handful of others who were gathered at the edge of the camp.

How can she walk away from her destiny? How can she choose to be content with so little when so much more awaits her?

Desire got up and went straight after her friend.

"You can't," she called out, "You can't just stop and settle here! You can't give up now. Don't do this! You'll have so many regrets later on." Shaking her head, she continued, "This place isn't safe. It's too close to where we came from."

Dawn stopped and turned to look at her.

Desire searched her friend's eyes, longing to capture any hint of reconsideration.

But there was no response. Dawn turned back and continued to limp towards the others.

Desire went over and put her hand on her shoulder.

"I'm not going to let you do this. Come on, I'm not going to leave you here." Desire's concern for her friend was bleeding out. She put Dawn's arm around her own neck for support as she attempted to walk her towards the land of their dreams in the west.

Dawn ducked out of her hold. Desire grabbed her arm anyway.

"Let me go!" Struggling to get free, Dawn slapped Desire's arm hard enough to leave a red mark. Desire quickly released her hold.

Dawn backed up, her mouth opened and her eyebrows raised. Even she was surprised at what she had done.

"I know you want to help, but, *please*, just let me be. You're stronger than I am, Desire; I can't be *you*. I just can't do it...there's enough for me here. Take care, I hope you find it." Dawn hobbled away. Desire's intense expression began to soften as she watched Dawn join the newly formed group of settlers.

Desire stood there with one hand over her mouth, paralyzed in disbelief. This was the second time she failed to convince an important person in her life to continue on to something more, first her father and now Dawn.

Desire was frustrated and confused. How could this be happening, especially after such an unbelievable escape? And why wasn't anyone else doing something to try to stop her and the others from settling?

Desire felt her neck tense up, her throat muscles begin to swell.

Sam walked over to her and put his hand on her shoulder. "You have to let her go. It's her choice."

Desire turned and looked at him. She was perplexed and irritated that he stood there and did absolutely nothing. She didn't say a word. He must have noticed her annoyance with him.

He went on, "It's good that you tried. We're sad to lose them too, but we need to move on. It's time to go."

With Sam by her side, Desire finally joined the Young Revolutionaries preparing to make their descent.

Dawn, and the group who became known as the Liberated, headed back the way they came. They planned to settle on the foothills of the Silver Mountains, right on the border of where the bronze dirt touched Freedom Mountain.

Desire's eyes were full as she walked down the mountain with Sam, replaying over and over again the conversation she just had with Dawn.

She was upset that Dawn decided to settle in a place so perilously close to the other kingdom.

Why Dawn would choose to live in such a vulnerable position, one where she would always have to be on guard in case King Laird recaptured her was completely unknown to Desire. She wondered if Dawn realized how close she would be sleeping to the enemy each night.

"I just don't get it. How could Dawn give up so soon... so soon after such a divine deliverance?" she asked Sam as they hiked down. "Her ankle would have healed soon enough. How could she settle right there, so near to that awful place? *I* want to get as far away as possible."

"I'm with you. I don't want to ever set foot near that place again," Sam replied.

"Well, can I ask you a question then?"

"Sure."

"Why didn't you do anything to try and stop her?!"

"Hmmm...I don't know, maybe Dawn and the others believe they are safe now that they are free. Maybe that's enough for them. Maybe Freedom Mountain is the most they can believe in for now. Sometimes we have to let people make their own decisions."

Desire raised an eyebrow. She was not convinced.

Sam looked up as if searching the sky for a more satisfying answer. "Hey, maybe she'll change her mind later and meet up with us farther down the way. It could happen."

Even though Desire was not persuaded at all by what Sam had said about just letting people go, walking with him helped her to be more at ease.

As they continued their descent down the other side of the mountain, Desire was intrigued by what she saw below.

Barrenness So Beautiful

The Barren Valley lived up to its name in every way. As far as Desire could see, there were only a few lonely trees scattered throughout the long valley. It reminded her of the miserable kingdom she had lived in just days before, and she estimated it would take at least a week before they reached the next mountain.

The Young Revolutionaries were making slow progress as they walked across the desolate place. The sun beat down on them in the day, and the cold pressed heavily on them during the night. After several days of traveling deep into the heart of the valley, the group was running low on their water supply and the few berries they had gathered on Freedom Mountain. Their lack of energy hindered their pace. Joshua had warned them that the journey would be difficult, even dangerous, and that was just how it was turning out. The valley would still take a long time to cross.

After just one week in the Barren Valley, rations of bread were dwindling. Each person received only one small portion a day. Desire's small figure was wasting away and she was getting weaker as were the others. She began to realize that there was a real possibility of starving to death out there. Lack of nourishment was making her delusional, even to the point of doubting the Legend at times. It was clear to her that the excitement of the journey had worn off in those around her and the drastic hunger affected some more than others.

"Why did you have to bring us out here anyway? I'm starving! Where's the food?" Desire's Aunt Clemente screamed at Joshua in camp one afternoon. Desire noticed the large dark circles under her aunt's eyes and an increasing number of wrinkles worn into her skin.

Desire's aunt was widowed after her husband stepped in to try and protect a child from a soldier's abuse. Shortly after that horrible event, she moved in to help raise ten-year-old Desire. When Desire was growing up, she felt her aunt tried too hard replace her mother, which caused tension. While Desire was glad her aunt had the courage to embark on their journey, she avoided her most of the time because she didn't want to have to deal with her constant nagging.

Desire watched Aunt Clemente look at Joshua, as if looking to him for salvation.

"Where's all the fruit you promised us in the Golden Pastures? I want some *now*. Even the porridge we had back there is better than the almost nothing we have here. I hate you Joshua. I hate you for bringing me here. Look at this valley. It's even uglier than the Bronze Hills. What Golden Pastures? That place probably doesn't even exist. It's probably just a figment of your family's imagination!"

Desire empathized with Joshua. She had experienced outbursts from her aunt in the past too, but at the same time, Aunt Clemente's words merely echoed what everyone else was thinking.

"You saw the miracle of deliverance. We'll get through this," Joshua said, attempting to reassure her.

"Who put you in charge anyway? You're just a boy. You aren't even old enough to be a leader. You're the reason we're all going to starve to death," Aunt Clemente said in a punishing tone.

She stepped close to Joshua and accused, "You've brought us here to die!"

Joshua went to put his hand on Aunt Clemente's shoulder. She batted it away, and then swung her arm at his head. He blocked her hand and stepped to the side. Desire had never seen her aunt swing at anyone before.

Desire felt sympathy for her aunt when she watched her look into Joshua's gentle and confused eyes, then turn and run away, hiding her face as she went. In that moment, it struck Desire that her aunt was the only family she had near her now. Desire decided to follow and sit beside her on the sandy ground. She felt it was time to get over the things from the past and to be there for her family. She didn't feel the need to say anything. She wanted her aunt to have someone present in her lonely state.

***

Initially, Desire noticed very little beauty in the Barren Valley. In her first week there, she thought it brought out the worst in people, as with Aunt Clemente. And for many of the others, it seemed that the divine sign of rescue had already begun to fade from their memories.

A few hours after the incident at camp, Desire saw Aunt Clemente approach Joshua. Before she had a chance to say anything, he gave her a hug and said that everything was okay. Desire was surprised that Aunt Clemente went to make things right. This was unusual behavior for someone who in the past would have only made things more difficult. It also amazed Desire that Joshua didn't take it personally, that he saw through the anger and fear and stepped out to offer love.

While in the valley, Desire discovered a hidden beauty in her fellow travelers. It took being in that place to reveal it. When nothing else was bright, when all she could see was desolation, she saw what she had never seen before. When she looked into her friends' eyes, she began to see something new. It was in that dark valley, in her desperate state of hunger, that she saw a deeper reflection of beauty in the others.

She noticed that because the Young Revolutionaries were forced to depend on each other for survival, they worked together more than before. Everyone pitched in to help gather the limited firewood, even Aunt Clemente lent a hand. Joshua and Sam reorganized their packs so they could carry more and help to lighten the load for Desire, her aunt, and some of the others. Blankets were shared during the cold nights. These little gifts of generosity made a big difference. The cold, the barrenness, and the hunger forced them to weave their lives together so that they could move toward their destinies.

One evening, Sam was sitting by Desire in front of the campfire when the subject of the Barren Valley came up.

"There's something so mystifying about being here. The desperation, humility, and brutal rawness of this place reveal the core of people's hearts more than before," Sam said.

"Everything does feel magnified here," Desire remarked.

She looked at him. He turned to face her.

She could almost feel his brown eyes penetrate through her own and into her heart when he said, "There's no way to hide who you really are in this valley."

This time, Desire didn't drop her eyes like she normally did during awkward moments. She held his gaze. There was something special about him that she had not noticed before. Finally, she grinned and stole her eyes back, returning to look at everyone else in the valley.

Her heart beat rapidly. She felt as if he was reading her soul, and she had the sense that he liked what he saw.

But wait a minute, this was Sam.

She had known him for several years and never saw him as anyone other than a good friend. Maybe it was the hunger that was making her more vulnerable than normal.

What was really going on here? Was this the beginning of love, was it infatuation, or was it just a moment that would quickly fade away?

Desire wasn't quite sure. She wondered if she was just imagining things.

Hesitation

After almost two weeks in the Barren Valley, Desire and the others finally made it to the next mountain. When she saw the blackberry bushes spotting the valley's edge, she ran over and frantically filled her mouth with the berries. After all the stale bread, the taste of something sweet recharged her. Sam also found pine nuts and brought some over to share with her. Joshua announced that they would spend the evening and the next day resting there and preparing for the climb ahead.

When the time came to climb the second mountain, the Young Revolutionaries worked together more than they had before. Desire noticed that Joshua and Kaden staggered themselves and set a pace for Aunt Clemente and some of the slower hikers, helping them ascend with fewer scrapes and bruises. It was refreshing for Desire to see that Kaden and some others had begun to realize that they were all on this journey *together* and that it didn't matter who was the first to get to the top.

When Desire reached the pinnacle of the second mountain, she could see the golden sun shining through the chain of Silver Mountains that lay ahead. The sunset was even more beautiful to her than the one she saw on Freedom Mountain. On the first mountaintop, the air was full of freedom. This time, there was something more in the air she breathed. The air on this mountaintop not only contained a new sense of freedom for Desire, but was also filled with a deeper appreciation for the others.

The strengthened bond she felt with the Young Revolutionaries while traveling through the Barren Valley also made Desire miss the deeper connection she could have had with Dawn. The empty space in her tent was a constant reminder that Dawn, along with the Liberated, were now farther away than ever before.

***

Weeks turned into months as she continued to climb mountains and endure the valleys below, but there was still no sight of the Golden Pastures. The more they moved west, the more the landscape on the mountains improved with apple trees as well as blackberry and raspberry bushes dotted throughout. Spring arrived, and she saw flowers spring up sporadically in the valleys and in small patches on the mountains.

But Desire, along with the other revolutionaries, became increasingly frustrated because they still had no idea how much longer their trip would be. Were the Golden Pastures just around the corner? Was the Legend just a fairy tale after all? Their hopes rose and were dashed several times a day as someone would have a feeling or catch a glimpse of what they thought might be the Pastures, simply to find it was only a mirage.

Desire wished her mind was playing tricks on her when she saw what came next in their travels. As she got closer, however, she saw that it was real in every way.

The magnitude of the mountain towering before her was breathtakingly daunting. The deeper and the more

barren the valleys were, the more immense the mountains became that followed them. As she approached the
one that stood before her, she saw intense silver sparkles
throughout its steep and almost vertical formation. Standing in its shadows, she felt insignificant. The rocky mountain itself commanded respect because of the extraordinary strategy and teamwork it would require to ascend.
This was the tallest barrier to climb since their journey
had begun several months before. There didn't seem to be
any way around it, or if there was, it was sure to lead them
away from the Pastures.

She looked at Joshua as he geared up for the climb.
The Young Revolutionaries prepared their packs for
the climb.

"I don't know about this," she said to Sam before
dropping her pack to the ground.

"Don't worry, you'll manage." Sam stood by her.

But what if she couldn't make it to the top of this
one?

She looked at Joshua as he geared up for the climb.
He caught her eye and then she saw him look down at her
pack. He came over to join her and Sam. He put his hand
in his back pocket and pulled out an old piece of paper.

"Take a look at this." He stood between Desire and
Sam. "You too, Sam," he said as he opened up the paper.
The bark-colored paper was wrinkled, creased, and worn,
like old maps pirates found in bottles, leading to buried
treasure.

Desire held one edge of the old drawing. He leaned
it in her direction. She focused in on the images she saw
there. Sam, looking agitated, peered over the left side of
her shoulder and put his head between theirs.

"Wow, so there it is?" Desire said pointing at the right side of the map.

Joshua nodded.

"Try not to lose sight of this, I know you can make it there," he said and then refolded and slid the map back into his pocket. This was not just any old map; this was *the* map that the Kane brothers left behind. It had been passed on through generations until it finally found its way into the hands of Joshua, a descendant of the family of Kane.

Desire was fascinated to think that the Kane brothers had taken this same journey hundreds of years before when they escaped and searched to find the land of their dreams. They had gone all the way until they found what they described as a land filled with fruit and abundance, the place they called "The Golden Pastures." When they snuck back into the Bronze Hills to share this great news, many did not believe them or were too intimidated by the king who ruled at the time to do anything about it. The few who were interested in going back with them lost all motivation after the brothers suddenly disappeared. The king, who was said to have been an ancestor of King Laird, heard that the sons of Kane were back and in hiding, and that they were stirring up the people to escape. Through the facts brought to him by his network of informers, he had them kidnapped, and they were never heard from again.

"I'll see you both over there," Joshua said before he walked toward the mountain.

The faded images of succulent pineapple, banana, and orange trees teeming from elaborate landscapes re-married Desire with the hope that one day she *could* experience the full life her heart longed to have. She imagined a plethora of colorful flowers, pomegranates, figs, and ripe fruits; grapes so plump that it would take two people to carry just one cluster of them. She imagined herself running barefoot in fields of wild flowers and glowing in the sunshine that would light up the land.

Sam asked her if she was ready to move on. She gathered her gear and they joined the others who were already moving toward the mountain's base.

The first few hours of their hike were filled with clear skies. As they carried on, Desire and the others encountered a dangerous and abrupt rock face. There on the side of the silver mountain was a steep wall of granite. Joshua and the more skilled rock climbers scaled to the top ledge and let a rope dangle down for the others. As Desire observed the daring mountaineers make their way up the perilous obstacle, she remembered Dawn's injury. Fear engulfed her.

Collision

"Desire, it's your turn," Sam said while holding out a rope.

"There must be some other way...around maybe? I mean, this can't be the *only* way up." Desire fumbled her words. This unexpected juncture unlocked her insecurities once again.

"This is it. There *is* no other way, I'm sorry. Just hang on tight." He brought the rope to tie her in. "I'll be here guiding you with my words and helping you know where to put your feet."

She swatted the rope away.

"What if something happens to me?"

"Don't worry. You made it this far, nothing's going to happen to you. Trust me, just hang on," Sam said. His eyes were so believable.

Desire looked around and saw that she either had to go up the vertical rock face to make it to the top or else retreat back down the mountain alone. There were no other options.

She let Sam secure the rope around her and then she took a deep breath before stepping forward toward the huge rock.

She held the rope and scrambled up the side of the mountain as Joshua and the others pulled from above. Hanging on to the threaded chord, she used her feet to guide her up. The voices below became gradually fainter the higher she went. This only added to the rising terror she felt. When she realized how high up she was, she started to shake. Her muscles tightened. She tried not to look down. She already knew she was in a hazardous position and didn't need to be reminded of that.

She placed her weight upon a small rock ledge. Suddenly, it crumbled beneath her foot and she lost all contact with the mountain. The abrupt change in slack caught the ones pulling her up by surprise. They quickly tightened the line, but her momentum caused her to swing into the side of the mountain, slamming her body hard against the rock's face. She felt as if the rope tied around her waist was about to strangle her in two. She dangled in the air, limp and in a state of shock.

Snapshot memories and faces of loved ones rapidly flashed through her mind. Her adrenaline skyrocketed. Her heart pounded. Her breathing was shallow and weak. She squeezed the rope tightly with both hands. This relieved some of the pressure from her stomach.

"Hang on. We'll pull you up. Take a minute if you need to. You're going to be alright," Joshua shouted down to her. "Just remember to breathe."

Her stomach was throbbing. She wondered if there was any way to make it up without being injured further. As she was being dragged up, she guided herself to get the fewest scrapes along the rock, but the shock of the near fall sapped almost all of her conscious energy. When they finally got her all the way up near the top, Joshua grabbed her hand and pulled her the rest of the way. He sat her down where it was safe.

"You okay?" Joshua asked. He must have known the answer already. She was not anywhere close to okay, physically or emotionally.

She was in shock. Her left hand was bleeding and her right hand was swollen and bright red from lack of circulation and rope burns. Her leg was peppered with abrasions and several deep cuts. Her stomach ached. The rest of her body was battered. She felt nauseous.

What if she died right then and there?

She wanted to be left alone.

"You're head's bleeding," Joshua noticed the cut and pressed some cloth against it.

After examining the wound, he said, "It's not that serious. You should be okay."

Some time passed before Sam finally made it up the steep rock. He found her right away.

"I'm so glad you were able to hang on. I was scared for you."

Desire couldn't get a word out. She was still shaken. She was angry because Sam was the one who told her she would be alright, that she would make it up safely. She felt lied to. She hadn't made it up safely like he promised. Instead, she crashed into side of the rock. What if she had blacked out when she hit her head?

He told her to trust him and she had. And look at what happened. *How dare he mislead me*, she thought. *It's his fault I'm in so much pain.*

She was angry at Joshua for encouraging her to continue on the journey. She was angry at herself for saying yes when it brought her this pain.

When the rest of the Young Revolutionaries made it to the top, Joshua said it would be best if they found a safe place nearby to set up camp so that Desire could tend to her wounds. He found some aloe leaves and squeezed their juices into her cuts then helped her to her tent. Kaden arranged Desire's pack and blanket to help her get as comfortable as possible. Physically and emotionally exhausted from the climb, Desire was in so much pain that it was hard for her to fully enter a deep, rejuvenating sleep, especially as the ground seemed harder than normal that night. She felt sore all over, and her stomach hurt every time she breathed. All she could do was lie there and pray for morning to come.

After the next day of resting, Desire agreed with the group that she was well enough to go forward. She didn't like the feeling of everyone waiting around on her account anyway. The near fall made her think more deeply about life than she had before. Even though she was making herself distant, Kaden told her to look at the bright side of things. Desire thought Kaden was a great friend but sometimes she just didn't get it, especially when the problem involved someone else's painful reality. It was as if Kaden was a perpetual optimist which sometimes made Desire want to be a perpetual pessimist just to wake her from her idealistic dream world.

Desire chose to hike on her own most of the afternoon because she was still unnerved and processing her near-death experience. She struggled along while Sam stayed behind to make sure she would make it up safely.

As they continued to climb and pace themselves, Desire felt a little better and decided to hike with Sam. She had trouble trusting him because he promised she would make it up the mountain safely and she didn't. She knew blaming him was irrational. Who could control a situation like that? But at the same time she hesitated to have full confidence in him. She was pushing him away when, secretly, all she really wanted to do was to have him hold her close.

Part Two

Metamorphosis

If I am already transformed
If I am already free
If I am already a beautiful butterfly, please let me
see
Open my eyes
Show me I don't have to live like a worm
I feel like one, but I am so unsure
Help me live free of the constraints of my cocoon

I am a new creation

Help me no longer crawl in the dirt
When You've called me to fly
Help me see my wings, help me believe they are
real
For I want to fly with You, coasting in Your love
I want to teach others to fly
Without You I don't know how
Lead me to the cliff where I must learn to soar
And rise above the clouds

-J.M.

Surrounded by the Middle

As Desire hiked further up the mountain that nearly took her life, she noticed something sparkling in the distance. Sam was close by and he saw it, too. She was drawn to the reflection on the peak, mesmerized by its brilliance. She couldn't make out what it was, and Sam didn't know either.

Silver granules were mixed in the dirt, and they became brighter and more common the closer she got to the mountaintop. There was something obviously different about this place. She couldn't explain it, but the alluring and almost magnetic force coming from the mountain's silver crest captivated her.

Her fascination with the peak made the long hike go by more quickly. Before she knew it, she and Sam approached the top in time to see the red and orange sunset that painted the sky. Below the peak, Desire saw several green trees laden with apples as well as several more scattered blackberry bushes.

The visibility was incredible that late afternoon. Rather than follow Sam as he walked to join the others at the camp, Desire took some time for herself to enjoy the view.

Looking to the east, she thought she could almost see to the end of the mountain chain and the Bronze Hills in the distance behind them. She couldn't believe that she had really inhabited that dreadful place for so many years. The contrasted beauty in the Silver Mountains made the Bronze Hills even more repulsive to her. She wondered if the mysterious army overthrew King Laird, if there was finally justice and equality in that dark place, if her father was okay. She just couldn't be sure one way or the other. Looking back only reminded her of how she longed to see her father's face.

***

Back in the Bronze Hills when she was younger, Desire used to count down the days until she was able see her father. Marks like those seen in prison cells covered the walls of her room and when that special day arrived, it was the best day of her life all over again. She used to stay up late, watching and waiting by the window, listening to every sound, trying to distinguish her father's footsteps until...Bam! She would run out and crash into his arms. He would walk slowly, with his head down, slouching and exhausted. But from the moment she jumped into his arms, he was transformed. He stood up straight, laughed, and played. He came alive for a few days out of the month whenever he saw her. When it was time for him to go back to work, the thought of being near the king caused him to hang his head again as he went back to that dreadful palace.

A week before she escaped, Desire was determined to convince her father to join her on the journey. When he finally came home that day, she ran out to meet him, filled with enthusiasm for the plan and talking so fast that he said he could barely understand a word she said. She eventually slowed down enough to explain the strategy they laid out.

"Dad, you *have* to come with us. I don't want be apart from you anymore. It'll be so much better there, I promise," she pleaded.

"Sweetheart, you know I can't leave," her father responded, worn out.

"But why? Why can't you leave? You hate your job. You hate this life here. Why stay?"

"This is my life now. I'm fine here. I'm not going... This is something your mother would have wanted to do, but it's not for me anymore. If this is something your heart is set on, that's fine, I support you. You know that."

Desire questioned, pleaded, and spent the whole night trying to get him to see, to hope, to risk again. The evening ended with his resolute answer. Nothing was going to change for him.

Aunt Clemente watched these conversations unfold without saying a word. She must have thought that if his own daughter couldn't convince him, there was no way that she could change his mind.

Before he returned to work the next day, Desire hugged him for what seemed like an eternity. She wasn't sure whether their lives would ever intersect again.

***

In that moment atop the mountain, Desire suddenly felt compelled to believe that somehow her journey with the Young Revolutionaries would one day reunite her with her father. She had no idea how they would be together again, but she felt a peace about her father that she had not felt before.

Still looking towards the east, she also saw Freedom Mountain. What an unforgettable night it was when she celebrated her new freedom with victory dances there. While it was great to see how far she had come, seeing that silhouette reminded her of the times she had with Dawn.

Desire was still disappointed that Dawn and the others who settled couldn't be with her to see the view from this enchanting mountain, so much more glorious than the view from all the other peaks thus far. She wanted to share the present moment with *them* as well. But they didn't come. She wondered if they would ever come.

Her moment of reflection there was more bitter than sweet. Overwhelmed by memories of loved ones who were now no longer a part of her life, she wished she could also be flooded with joy. But she wasn't, and she couldn't fake that emotion. She thought it would be wise not to spend too much time looking back until the time was right. She didn't feel strong enough to handle the burden that came with that kind of reflection.

Desire's future beckoned her onward. When she turned toward the west, she saw a golden horizon. Seeing a glimpse of what she hoped was truly the Pastures strengthened her belief in the Legend even more. Even though it seemed that they were only about halfway there and that it would still take more time, it was a refreshing sight to see. She imagined hills covered with green trees and fields filled with red, yellow, and blue flowers. She imagined the full life that her heart longed to embrace.

After being drawn to the Pastures for what seemed like hours, she turned her head to camp and caught sight of Sam. His whole body looked slightly silver, and his face reflected the color. Desire wondered what the change in Sam was. She walked over to him. Even though he was in the midst of a conversation, he left the others and came to meet her. He couldn't hold back his excitement. With a little hop, he exclaimed,

"I can't believe the view from here! This feels *so* good! And it feels so good to be around you, too." He looked into her eyes. "I'm so glad you're here." They were a little distance from the others when he put his arms around her. He held her close and neither of them pulled back from the embrace. People were near enough to see them, but for some reason, it didn't bother her this time. She had been comfortable with him before, but this was something different.

Desire finally released her hold, but he didn't let go. Still in his arms, their eyes met. The uncomfortable silence seemed to last longer than the hug.

"Goodnight," she couldn't handle the growing tension, she broke away from him. She went to find Kaden so they could set up their tent. When she looked back at Sam, she saw him standing there, watching her as she left. Her heart began to race. She tried to mute the voice in her head that said over and over again that Sam liked her. She knew the safest thing for her to do would be to go on pretending that they were just friends. That way she wouldn't get hurt again as she had in her past relationship when she was abandoned.

Luckily, Kaden wasn't in sight when they hugged or else she might have asked Desire twenty questions that night. After the two set up their tent, they ate soup and some of the ripe apples before they headed for bed. It took Desire a while to settle down enough to relax. She feared that falling asleep that night would take a lot of work; the chaotic energy inside of her was bursting to express itself. As she attempted to get comfortable, she tried to convince herself that everything that had happened earlier with Sam was all in her head.

Heart of Clay

The next day, Joshua announced to the Young Revolutionaries that he thought it best to set up a more stable camp there for a while, at least a month or so. He said it would be wise to spend some time storing up food for the long journey ahead. The rest would also give them time to get rejuvenated. He said he wanted to make sure they were better prepared so they wouldn't run out of food like they had before in the Barren Valley. Desire saw her aunt grin with relief at Joshua's request.

Desire didn't mind staying there either, she wasn't in a hurry. She enjoyed the view, and the apples and pine nuts there were good to eat. Besides that, temporarily slowing down the pace of life would also give her the opportunity to get to know Sam better.

After gathering berries each day, Desire spent all her spare time with Sam. She missed him when she didn't see him, which wasn't that much. Sometimes she wanted to get him out of her head so she could think about anything else, but most of the time, if she was honest with herself, she couldn't shake the consuming thoughts of him that flooded her mind day and night.

A couple of weeks into their stay on the mountaintop, Sam approached Desire while she was picking blackberries with Kaden and some of the others. Desire noticed him coming and saw that he avoided eye contact with her.

Something must be going on. Suddenly, she felt a nervous anxiety sweep through her stomach.

When he made it to her, he leaned over and said, "Can I talk to you?"

Kaden looked at them.

"Okay, should we go for a walk?" Desire tried to remain calm and cool.

"That would be great," he said as they walked away from where the others were picking berries.

"How's it going with the shelters?" she asked.

"Good. It's good."

An awkward silence accompanied them on their walk for some time before Desire finally broke in.

"So, what's on your mind?"

It took a few moments before he finally said, "You know, um, I really like that, uh, you're here with us." She could see him squirming.

"I'm happy to be here now, too," she answered.

"Well...um...I'm beginning to realize that you mean a lot to me. I feel alive when I'm with you."

Excitement and fear engulfed her. She wanted to run away, to crawl in a hole and hide somewhere.

Sam turned and took hold of her hand. "I want us to be together."

Desire suddenly felt weak. Her face turned bright red. She always thought she was the more upfront person of the two, but now Sam spelled everything out so simply. His words made her want to run away even more. She felt overwhelmed with too much love.

"Oh Sam, I don't know." She hesitated. It wasn't that she didn't care for Sam. She did. It was just that she didn't

want the same thing to happen to her as before. She was
still tending wounds from the betrayal of someone in her
past who had spoken similar words. She was afraid of being vulnerable again, of needing someone, of giving another person the power to hurt her again.

"It could work. I know this could work," he said.

"I just need some time to think about this. I mean,
we've been good friends for so long."

Desire was unsure. Diving into a relationship with
him could potentially ruin their friendship. Of course she
didn't want that. Once that line was crossed with Sam,
there was no going back, and things would get serious very
quickly. Was she really ready to jump into something like
this?

"Okay, if that's what you want," Sam said. Withdraw-
ing his hand from hers, he said he would give her the room
she needed to make up her mind.

Think about it she did. It kept her up most of the
night. Her mind was spinning. Instead of mere daydream-
ing as it had been before, she thought about a real relationship with someone who appeared to care for her deeply.
That night, Kaden asked about her conversation with
Sam. Desire told her that she wasn't ready to talk about it.
She wanted to make up her mind about Sam first before
hearing what others had to say. Kaden let it go, and Desire
was relieved.

The next day, when Desire went out to pick apples,
her focus was gone. She sat and stared at the trees without
realizing how much time had passed. She kept to herself in
the evening. She didn't want to make a huge mistake with
Sam or jump into anything she would later regret. That

whole day and night though, all she could think about was Sam. It was as if almost overnight their relationship had completely shifted.

She went to bed early that evening, hoping a good night's sleep would do her some good. Unfortunately, another restless night ensued.

"Can I talk to you for a minute?" Desire approached Sam the following morning. He immediately excused himself from a conversation to go on a walk with Desire.

Sam's face was filled with uncertainty. She knew he had no idea which way their relationship would go. They walked casually before Desire gained enough courage to speak.

"How have you been?"

"Good. You?" he replied as normally as possible.

"I've been fine."

"Good," Sam said.

"Yeah." Desire was uncomfortable. She wondered how much longer she could continue with small talk.

"Well…" she said before pausing. Their pace slowed to a standstill. She turned to him. "I'm sorry for making you wait. I just needed some time to think about all that you said."

Sam waited. Desire saw him look at her and then look down.

"I'd like to try to see if things might work out with us…" She finally verbalized the words she had wanted to say to him.

His face lifted up with a smile.

Desire's heart leapt inside of her.

"But I'm scared," she said before continuing. "The first day we met, I felt comfortable around you...and lately I've been thinking about you, too." Did she really just say that out loud and not only admit it to herself but also to the *boy* standing in front of her?

Sam stepped closer. There was nowhere else for her to go. Nowhere else she wanted to go. He initiated the hug. She melted into him. She didn't want to let go, she felt safe and loved in those arms. He pulled back slightly and said, "I want to be with you. I can't handle going this long without seeing you. These last two days have been torture."

She was lost in his gaze. He leaned in. His lips touched hers. As she felt him kiss her softly, her heart was ignited. On the outside she remained calm, yet on the inside, her heart was flying. It felt so natural and so good to be with him, to be in his embrace.

Colors Clash

Desire and Sam snuck away from their tasks of gathering food and collecting wood to go for a long hike together. It was Desire's idea. She spent much of that day hand in hand with Sam, enjoying every moment of his company.

Later that night when Kaden asked where she had disappeared to, Desire told her all about Sam.

"I knew it. I saw it coming," Kaden said. "It's like a dream come true for you," she added. Needing to know every detail from start to finish, from their initial words on the subject to their first kiss, Kaden did not let Desire sleep until she heard all the high points in their budding relationship. After all the excitement, they finally calmed down enough to sleep.

During the days that followed on that silver capped mountaintop, Desire regained courage to risk again and to open up to Sam. After their daily tasks, they could rarely be seen apart in the evenings.

Desire enjoyed her new lifestyle there. She had everything she needed; she had Sam and their relationship was good, she had berries and apples to eat besides the soups they made, and she had a nice community surrounding her. Her body had healed from the fall as well. And besides all this, the view was great. She thought that Middle Mountain was the perfect resting place. Life was peaceful there with no real worries. They had even built wooden coverings over their tents for a more secure shelter.

As Desire spent more time with Sam, she thought less and less of the Golden Pastures. He didn't talk much about them anymore either. Instead, he spoke about the beauty he could actually see on the silver mountain. At the time, it didn't really bother her because she believed that things would change when it was time to go. His dedication to reach the Pastures would rekindle, she just knew it. She did notice though, that Joshua's passion to reach the Pastures was still alive and thriving.

Just over a month had passed on the mountain when Joshua told the others he had a sense it was time to move on. He said they had gathered enough fruits and nuts to help them through the next stage of the journey. Many of the others agreed, and they decided they would pack up camp and leave in three days.

After Joshua made the announcement, Desire noticed Sam acting differently towards her. He was quieter than normal and he even avoided her in the evenings, which he hadn't done before. Believing it might just be a phase he would soon snap out of, she decided to let it go. Deep down, though, she felt something might be wrong.

As the morning of descent came, Sam pulled Desire aside and said,

"I need you to know that I really like it up here. We're far enough away from the Bronze Hills to be safe and secure. Several of the others feel comfortable on this mountain as well."

Desire looked at him and feared where this conversation was going. With a hurry-up-and-get-to-the-point look, she crossed her arms, raised an eyebrow and uttered in an emotionless tone, "Okay?"

"Being here all this time has helped me remember how nice it feels to just stop and settle. I'm so tired of always being on the go. Setting up, and then tearing down camp, just to do it all over again. I just want to 'be,' I don't want to pack and unpack anymore. I need to unpack for good." He looked into her eyes. "I want to build a life here, a family...with you."

A dead silence fell between the two of them.

She was stunned and attempted to process what was said. This must be the reason she had felt distant from him the past few days.

Words finally fell off her lips, "But I thought you believed in the Legend too."

"I do...well, I did. But what if the Legend already served its purpose to bring us here?" he asked.

"But I know this isn't *it*," she said while at the same time realizing he had a point. She *did* have everything she needed there: a man who loved her, enough food, shelter, and security.

Maybe the Legend did serve its purpose in getting us this far. Maybe this was good enough.

Desire was confused; it was all happening too quickly.

Why didn't he speak to me about this before? Why did he have to wait until the very last minute to bring this up?

"There's so much more awaiting us if we keep moving forward, I just know it," she said. "We're so close. We can practically see the—"

"But there's no guarantee we'll even make it to the Pastures...I'm ready to settle here, now. This mountain has just what we need for that." Taking her hands, he said, "Desire, let's stay here together."

She felt trapped, knowing she needed to move quickly but not sure which way. Should she stay there with someone whom she could see a real potential in settling down with one day? Or should she go where her heart had been leading her all along, with Joshua, Kaden, and the others on an exciting but dangerous adventure to an unknown place where she *might* find that full life she had always hoped for?

The tug of war going on in her heart was pulling her in both directions. She wondered why she couldn't have both of those things. That would solve her problem. She knew her life would look drastically different depending on which direction she chose.

"But you've made it so far already. This isn't you. This can't be us," she said.

Joshua approached the two of them. He must have overheard her concern.

Desire dropped Sam's hands.

"She's right. This mountaintop isn't it, and you're already halfway there. You don't have to choose this." Sam looked at him with a slight glare and then brought his focus back to Desire.

"Sam, you know it, too. This isn't it. This isn't our destiny. This isn't where we're supposed to end up. If this mountaintop is more beautiful than the ones we've encountered so far, then the Golden Pastures *must* be even greater," Desire said, gaining confidence from Joshua's presence.

"But this place is good. It may not be as wonderful as we imagine the Pastures to be, but it's still nice here," Sam said as he looked only at Desire. Joshua got the hint and backed out of the conversation. Sam continued speaking with Desire, "I'm just so tired of struggling forward, of risking without the security of knowing for sure if it will all work out like we imagine."

Sam persisted to display his resolve in a sympathetic tone. "Let me build a home for you here. I'll provide for you and keep you safe. You won't have to climb high mountains anymore."

He reached for her hands again. She felt his eyes become lost in the sea of her own. "Desire, stay here with me."

It's Difficult to Say

Desire melted inside. She couldn't hide the longing and desperation on her face. She had always wanted to be cherished, to have someone look at her the way he did, to be wanted. Sam would make a good husband, keep her safe and secure. What every young woman wants so badly, she literally had at her fingertips. Oh, the words she longed to hear: "Desire, stay with me." Yet she was not expecting to hear them so soon. And why *here*? Why now?

"Sam, you know I want to be with you, but not in this place, not this fast. You know I can't stop here."

At that, she saw his shoulders slouch and every sign of hope disappear from his face.

"I'm sorry, but I need to stay here...I want to stay here." Even though it was plain to see how much it would hurt her, he kept his position. He obviously wanted that more than he wanted to be with her. "I see things differently now. I'm honestly happy here. I don't need to go any farther." Squeezing her hands, he continued, "Are you *sure* you don't want to stay here...with me?"

She saw that the others were waiting for her.

"You *know* I can't. I can't live always wondering, 'what if?' Take good care of yourself and the others. You know where I'll be if you change your mind."

He looked into her eyes, she held back their flow. She loosened her hands then threw them around his neck, holding him closely. This might be the last time she would ever see him. She didn't want to let go, but she knew she had to.

A "goodbye" finally escaped from her lips before she tore herself away from him. She walked towards the others as they departed down the mountain. She didn't have the strength to look back; it was too painful for her to see Sam one last time.

"Goodbye," he called after her, watching the so-called love of his life depart. He stood motionless as Desire descended with the others. He let her go without chasing after her. If his heart did long for him to run after her, he took no action. His feet were stuck, glued to Middle Mountain. It was as if the silver on the mountaintop hypnotized and seduced him and the others, the Secured, to stop and settle there. Sam loved the comfort of that place more than he loved her. His actions told the tale.

A song Desire heard when she was younger helped connect her to the pain she was feeling as she walked on.

It's difficult to say goodbye after only one life.
The rain will fall down, replenishing all of our broken dreams.
And this burning tree that's withering will bloom again, would you believe?
Goodbye.
Walk away. It's time to say goodbye.
Now all that's left are pictures on the walls
Memories and stories that are told.
The more often told the bigger they get.
Create a legacy, lest we forget.
Goodbye.

Walk away. It's hard to say goodbye.
No longer can I hold on to this defeated change in heart
I swear
It's time to say "fare thee well" to life as we know it.
My voice it will be still.
Something woke me up in the midst of dream and fantasy,
Half way there.
But He always fills my cup.
And He lifts me up, oh how He lifts me up
Goodbye.
Walk away. It's time to say goodbye.
I never took the time to stop and realize that death takes many forms.
*Even while alive**

During their long descent down the mountain, Desire walked with her head down, fighting hard to hold in the tears. Sam's resolve to put down roots *there* injured her deeply. How could she not take it personally? She had spent so much time thinking about him, wondering what their future might hold. He was the stable one, the one who could protect her and provide for her. It hurt her to know that even after he had come so far, he chose to settle for less than the full life in the Golden Pastures. She couldn't understand his choice, especially after *he* had seen *her* struggle, after *he* had helped *her* make it up so many mountains.

Why couldn't he do this for me? He said he loved me, why didn't he fight for me, why didn't he come with me?

She replayed the scene with Sam over and over again in her head. Doubts and questions plagued her.

Did I just make a huge mistake? Should I have stayed with him? But how could I go back and be with him, knowing that the vision within my heart for the full life would never become a reality? But is it really going to be worth it in the end to live in the Pastures without him? Or would living with him on Middle Mountain make me forget all about the Pastures in the first place? Am I mad for following this Legend that sometimes seems so real to me and at other times seems like a complete fantasy? I can't believe I left him. I can't believe what we had is over.

Desire was lagging behind the group as they went down the mountain. Joshua came back for her.

"How are you doing?"

She barely looked up.

"I know it's tough," he said. "Don't give up. You'll be taken care of. I know that it'll take some time to get over losing Sam, but we'll be here for you." Her eyes began to fill. She clenched her teeth, not wanting her pain to spill over. Joshua stepped forward to console her, and she held him tight.

Desire let out, "This trip is too difficult. It's too hard. Why can't I just quit? Why won't this burning in my heart for the Golden Pastures just go away? Why can't I deny its persistent tug? And why so many sacrifices?" It was his brotherly hug that gave her the freedom to be vulnerable in his presence.

Joshua listened to her, offering no solutions. In the stillness, questions continued to tear at her heart.

What will happen if I endure all of this, get to the Golden Pastures, and am still not completely satisfied? Are the Pastures the place where I'm actually going to feel free and be fully content or is there any way to achieve that here and now, in the present journey and in all the places on the way? Why did Sam have to stay? I hate my life without him now. I thought that following the Legend would bring fulfillment and happiness, yet I suddenly feel more lost and confused than when I started.

After several moments of comforting her, Joshua asked if she was ready. She wiped her tears and they caught up with the others. Desire calmed down after being able to vent her feelings to one who cared. She wanted to be heard, to have someone who understood what she was feeling. She wanted to be loved again.

Separation

As they hiked through the next valley that began at the base of Middle Mountain, thoughts of Sam continued to overwhelm Desire as she mulled over her decision.

Did I really make the right choice? What if I never find anyone else to share my life with? What if being with Sam was my last chance of settling down and having a family one day? That's a dream in my heart too, but the timing feels so wrong. And even if I did change my mind, already now, even after only a few days, Sam and I are on two different paths. But the halfway point wasn't a fork in the road; it was a rest stop where he chose to make his permanent home. Rest stops are for rejuvenating, so we have more strength to continue in the journey. Why didn't Sam see that? I know I'm being selfish, but I miss him so much.

Desire had finally started to hope, to dream of a future with him, but then he decided to settle. He chose a different path. He left her, or she left him. It really didn't matter now because he had stayed behind. She had envisioned a future with him, but being with him there was not part of the journey, not part of the plan, at least not now.

She felt he could have been a good match for her. He would have brought stability and security to her. He had comforted her when she was upset. He had believed in her. He had looked and acted like the real thing and he seemed to fit the part. Well, he *almost* fit the part. He wasn't go-

ing where her heart was taking her, and it didn't appear
that he was following his own. He had fit her perfect little
imaginary box, but if she had been honest with herself before, she might have admitted that something wasn't quite
right, although, at the time, she couldn't name it.

And how could she live honestly before others if she
had stayed behind with Sam, if she had settled into a relationship where she felt trapped, felt like she was suppress-
ing who she was meant to be? She had to let go of him if
she was going to move on. She was compelled to live an
honest life, to be true to her dreams, true to her heart. She
couldn't settle for less than all that the Legend promised.
She couldn't deny the stirrings in her heart. If she stayed
with Sam on Middle Mountain, what depth of inspiration,
what powerful truth would she have to share with people?
How would she ever be able to inspire others to live their
dreams if she failed to fulfill her own deep-seeded dream
all because of another person? That's what she wanted,
and that's why she let him go.

She cared for him deeply, but she still felt betrayed.
She had opened herself up and been vulnerable with him,
shared her hopes and her fears. Yet he chose comfort over
being with her; the coward. Bitterness raged in her heart.
She wondered if their relationship was ever meant to go
further, if what they had was even real.

She felt numb and dead inside. She wondered why
pursuing the full life in the Pastures had to be so painful.
She wondered if there was any other way. Desire spent so
much time the last couple months with only Sam that she
had become so detached from everyone else. She even felt
out of touch with herself.

Revelation

With Sam and the other twenty settled into the security of Middle Mountain, the group of Young Revolutionaries was reduced to about forty people. With fewer people on the journey now, Desire was forced to get to know some of the others who were lost in the crowd earlier on. Victoria had been on the trip from day one, but Desire didn't talk to her much before because Victoria was always with her best friend. It was only after her friend decided to stay back with Sam and the Secured that their paths crossed more closely.

"Mind if I hike with ya today?" Victoria approached Desire one morning when they prepared to climb the next mountain on their way to the Pastures.

"Sure." Desire welcomed the company. Being mostly on her own while walking through the valley, she had too much time to think about Sam.

"How ya doing with it all?" Victoria asked as they walked. Everybody had witnessed Desire's goodbye to Sam.

"It's still hard," Desire said.

"Know what ya mean. I lost my best friend back there, too."

"Sorry to hear that," Desire said.

"So you were pretty close to him then?" Victoria asked.

Desire took a minute to reflect before answering, "I thought I was...Anyway, so who else is in your tent now?"

"Just me after my friend stayed back."

"You okay on your own?"

"To be honest, it's been gettin' kind of lonely these past couple of weeks without anyone in there."

"Oh."

"That's okay, I'll be alright," Victoria said.

"Well, we have an extra place in our tent. If you want to join, you are more than welcome."

"That would be nice. Sure ya don't mind?"

"It's no trouble at all, I'm sure Kaden will be fine with it, too."

***

Getting to know Victoria was a good distraction to help Desire keep her mind off of Sam. She had some good days and some bad ones as she moved on. She still looked back often in the hope of seeing Sam come running after her. Nevertheless, she continued to hike farther away from Sam and closer to the Golden Pastures.

Desire could hardly believe Victoria's story as it unfolded one evening when the girls stayed up chatting in their tent. Curious to know more about her, Desire asked how she chose to come on this journey in the first place.

"Always wanted to get out of the Bronze Hills," Victoria responded. "Weird, though, how I always felt this awful connection with King Laird. And he would regularly help my family for some reason. Couldn't understand why he did it and it felt so manipulative. That is, until just a few weeks before the escape, then my mom couldn't keep it a secret any longer."

"What happened?" Kaden asked.

"Everything made sense after that conversation, but I'm still trying to process it all. It's a lot to take in all at once. But ya both have to promise not to tell anyone. I've only told a few other people about this. Ya promise?"

Desire and Kaden both nodded their heads, "We promise."

"Please don't hate me."

Surprised, Desire looked at Kaden then back at Victoria, "No, we won't hate you."

Both Desire and Kaden leaned in.

"King Laird is my father." Victoria's words sliced through the anticipatory silence that her secret had created inside the tent.

"What?!" The girls were stunned.

"I know, I was shocked, too...*And*, my dad doesn't even know that he's not my real father. My mom made me promise not to tell him; said it would break his heart if he found out."

"How?" Desire asked.

"One day when my mom was cleaning inside King Laird's castle, he liked what he saw and took it, threatened to kill my family if she told anyone. So how's that for family secrets swept under the rug?!"

"I'll say!" Kaden said.

"That's awful. So are you okay?" Desire said.

"All right," Victoria said as she shrugged her shoulders. There was nothing she could do about it then anyway.

Victoria must have still been in denial over the whole thing. Desire couldn't see how anyone could be okay after finding out something so horrible. She knew that if something like that ever happened to *her*, she would be completely devastated. Needless to say, that information was a lot for her to swallow. It made Desire appreciate that even while her father was not with her, at least she knew who he was and that he was a good man.

As they continued toward the Pastures, the weather was getting warmer and summer was beginning to show its true colors. After several more weeks of traveling, Desire approached something she had long dreamed of seeing...

Dream

Was this really the Last Mountain they would have to climb? She trusted Joshua would know the answer.

"This is it, we've almost made it!" shouted Joshua. Shouting was a rare thing for him to do. The only other times Desire remembered hearing him shout were on the battlefield during their escape and when she was hanging on the side of the mountain.

"According to the map, the Pastures should be just on the other side. I recognize this mountain from my dreams," he said.

"Really?! This is so exciting," Kaden said.

"Oh, we're so close," Desire said.

"Finally, we're here!" Victoria beamed.

Disengaged from lingering thoughts of Sam, Desire skipped to the mountain giddily, eager to scale it as quickly as possible. Anticipation hurried her steps as she engaged in this final climb.

"I can't believe after all this time that we're almost there," Desire said to Kaden as they hiked up the mountain together.

"I know, this is so great," answered Kaden.

"It's been a long journey, hasn't it?" Desire said.

"It has."

"It'll be worth it, though," Desire said. "Just think, soon we'll get to eat pomegranates, oranges, grapes, and we'll be able to enjoy all that the Legend has promised about that land."

"Yeah, but I don't really need *all* that," Kaden said as she put out her hand to help Desire up a steeper part of the mountain.

Desire grabbed her arm and made it up to her.

"But don't you *want* it?" Desire asked.

"I guess so, but it's really all too much for me," Kaden said.

"Oh well, I guess you can take what you like and leave the rest," Desire said with a shrug of her shoulders.

"Guess so," Kaden said.

"Anyway, it's going to be so great, I can't wait."

"Yeah...Me neither."

With careful teamwork, Desire, Kaden, Victoria, and the others reached the mountaintop before sundown of the second day. The peak afforded them with the view for which they had dreamed, hoped, toiled and suffered. They made it to the summit in time to get a first glimpse of their promised land before the darkness hid it for the night.

Kaden leaned forward and put her hands on her knees.

"Wow! It's really there. It's almost too good to be true," Kaden said, looking down at the welcome mat of colorful plants. There were orange trees on the edges of the Pastures and an array of flowers patterned throughout the landscape.

"Wow is right," Desire said while taking it all in. "I can't believe how close we are now." She gave Kaden's arm a gentle squeeze.

"It might just be my imagination, but I think I can even smell the citrus from the orange trees down there," Kaden said, smiling at the panorama before them.

"After so long, it's finally happening," Desire said. She had never seen a land so kissed with an abundance of fruit and plant life.

The Legend was true after all. Desire knew it would be, but to actually see it with her own eyes astounded her.

Later that evening, as everyone gathered around the fire, Desire noticed that Kaden was missing. Scanning the group, she caught Victoria's eyes and searched them for information. Desire silently mouthed Kaden's name until Victoria caught on. Victoria pointed away from their bright circle, into the darkness of the night.

Desire found Kaden sitting down on a ridge that overlooked the moonlit Pastures. She walked over to her friend and laid a hand on her shoulder.

"Hey," she said in a soft tone.

Kaden looked back. Desire saw that she was on the verge of tears.

"Do you mind if I join you?"

Kaden shook her head.

Desire sat down beside her. Her own eyes softened as well. She looked at her and waited.

Finally Kaden burst out, "I think I'm going crazy. I mean, just look!" Kaden stretched her hand out over the darkened view. "It's more amazing than anything I could have ever imagined. And those trees and that fruit and,

and..." Both of Kaden's arms were now spread wide, highlighting the expansiveness of it all. She shook her head and then let out a deep breath as she let her arms fall to her sides.

"I'm...I'm scared. I'm scared the journey will end there, and I feel that I'm, well...that I'm not worthy of that land. I mean, who am *I*? What makes me so deserving of life in the Pastures? I just don't think I can handle the weight and the responsibility and..." She shook her head again. The moisture in her eyes spilled over. "I just don't know what to do."

Desire was not used to seeing Kaden's emotions on display.

"It will all work out," Desire said, wrapping an arm around her friend.

Kaden sat there for a few moments.

She wiped her tears before saying, "Yeah, maybe I just needed to hear that...So, the tent's all set up, right?"

Desire nodded, "We're just over there near my aunt's tent. You'll be okay, really you will be."

"I know. You're right."

After they chatted for a little while longer, Desire went back to their tent. Kaden took some more time for herself before heading back to camp.

When morning came, Kaden said a quick hello before exiting the tent early.

Not long after, Desire heard commotion in the camp. She immediately recognized the voices and got up to see what was going on.

A Fantastic Reality?

Squinting from the bright morning sunshine, Desire nearly ran into her Aunt, who grabbed her arm to steady her. She leaned in and said to Desire, "Kaden's breaking off from the group to stay here."

Desire's raised eyebrows and dropped jaw mirrored her Aunt's expression. The two watched from a distance as Joshua raised his voice through the thin mountain air.

"Our final stop is *there*, not *here*," he said to his sister.

"But if I go there, into that amazing place, what will come next, what else will I have to hope for?"

"But that's *where* your hopes will be realized, that's *where* you'll thrive," Joshua answered.

"But that's what I'm scared of. I'm not ready for what that will mean, for what that will look like, for how much that will change me. It's just too much for me right now."

Desire couldn't believe what she was hearing. Surely Kaden couldn't be talking about giving up *now*. Stopping this close to the Pastures would be ridiculous.

Besides, Kaden was the dreamer. She was the one who held tightly to the Legend of the Golden Pastures throughout the whole journey. Someone else might want to settle, but not Kaden. Desire never once heard her complain despite the many opportunities to do so. Kaden was instrumental in swaying the group to embark on the journey in the first place. It was she who took the crucial stand to support her brother when they all met a month before the escape.

***

"We'll work together. The timing's right, I can feel it so strongly. What do you say?" Joshua said to the nearly hundred packed into Sam's small brick home in the Bronze Hills. The entire group was frozen, paralyzed by fear. Slowly, they began to glance at each other through the dim candlelight. Joshua persisted,

"How can you be content to stay here? Now's our time to break out." Examining the crowd, he held his gaze for moments at a time, looking directly into the eyes of those gathered.

"Who's with me? I know the way." Joshua pronounced, holding up the weathered map in his tight fist. "This will lead us to our destiny!"

The room vibrated with murmurs before someone shouted out,

"It's too dangerous! We'll never make it out alive."

Emboldened by the articulation of their fears, others began to chime in as well.

"It's impossible," one said.

"How are we going to escape without them knowing?"

"We need more time to prepare."

Then, stepping out from the shadows, Kaden spoke up.

"Listen everyone, Joshua's right. If we don't go now, there will always be another excuse; we aren't prepared enough or the timing's not right or whatever else it might be. When will we ever really be prepared enough for something like this?"

After a momentary silence in the group, Victoria said, "She's got a point."

"That's right," another agreed.

"I feel drawn to the Pastures, too. I know some of you must feel it as well!" Kaden said.

"It's now or never, who's in?" Joshua said.

Heads began to nod, some hesitantly, but nonetheless most of them were in.

***

Desire put her folded hands to her lips as she watched Joshua continue to speak to his sister in a fatherly tone.

"We're family, we need to stay together. You'll be able to handle it. You've sacrificed and endured so much for this, don't sabotage it now."

"I know. I want to stay with you, but...I'm just not ready to see the fulfillment of the Legend. I need it to stay alive in me, to always have something to hope for. Seeing my dream come true would be like death to me. I need to see the vision beyond the Pastures for me to be able to go any farther...I can manage to live here. I'll eventually be okay."

"You can't be serious!" Lifting his hands, he exploded, "You'll *eventually* be *okay* here? You're within a couple days' journey from what you've worked so hard for and traveled so long to enjoy yet you say you can *manage* to be okay here? I know you'll be able to handle it over there, you'll see. Don't quit right before the finish line!" Desire had never seen Joshua speak so passionately before.

"Your expectations are just too high for me, Joshua," Kaden answered back.

Joshua's voice softened, "I want you to have the best life possible, that's all. We both know that your heart is not leading you here, to this mountaintop. It's leading you over there."

"I know, but I just can't say yes to you this time. I'm not ready...I'm sorry."

"*Please* tell me that you're not choosing this. Your dream is right there," Joshua said, pointing towards the Golden Pastures. "Take hold of it!"

"I can't, I told you," she said as she looked him straight in the eyes. "It's too much for me right now."

Desire's hands fell to her side. It was all over. Their family would be split apart. Desire felt like her family was being split apart too. After months of hardships and hopes, struggles and triumphs, Kaden had become like a sister to her. Desire watched Joshua hug his sister and then walk on. In a weird way, Desire was glad Joshua was the one to confront his sister. After losing Sam, she wasn't sure she had the strength to try to convince Kaden anyway. When Kaden approached her next, all Desire had left to give was a tight embrace and a "good luck" whispered in her ear.

Desire watched Kaden and the small group of ten, who became known as the Dreamers, start to set up a permanent camp on the Last Mountain. Desire couldn't understand how Kaden could be content to enjoy only a *view* of the Golden Pastures. She couldn't comprehend how Kaden could stay there, dreaming and fantasizing about what the future held, while not moving one step closer to it.

Regardless of the shock of Kaden and the Dreamers settling on the Last Mountain, Joshua, Desire, and the remnant of Young Revolutionaries packed their bags and continued to journey on.

Numbering thirty after the others had all settled in their new homes, they managed to make it more than halfway down the mountain before the sun was setting. They set up camp on a safe but rocky ledge on the mountainside, overlooking the green meadows in the Pastures. After organizing her tent with Victoria's help, Desire found Joshua. Even though she could see the Pastures then, she still wanted some reassurance.

"We're really here?"

Looking worn and heavy hearted, he nodded in the affirmative. He was in the middle of setting up his tent, but he stopped for a moment.

"You did it, Desire. Even after your near fall, everything with Sam...and even with my sister giving up. I'm really proud of you, really proud," Joshua said with a tone of sincere admiration in spite of his visible exhaustion.

"Thanks...I only wish that Kaden had made the same decision," Desire said.

"She'll eventually come around. Hopefully, it's just a matter of time for her," Joshua said as if he needed to hear those words for himself.

"How are you doing with it all?"

"Truthfully, I'm devastated. It breaks my heart to see my sister stay behind...One day she'll be ready to take the next step, though."

"I hope for that, too."

Desire helped him set up his tent, and they talked for a little while before she went to her tent for the night.

Desire still held firmly to the hope that she would see her friends who had settled, that one day they would change their minds and come to meet her in the Golden Pastures. It was this hope that helped her reconcile herself with Kaden's decision to stop short. Still eager for the rest of the trip, images of the Golden Pastures filled her mind as she struggled to fall asleep. Would she wake up and find that it was all just a dream?

Part Three

Generously

Soaring above the clouds I am
In the sunlight of Your beauty I make
Circles of freedom in Your love
Capturing the glory inside me
Rainbow shouts from my heart
Coloring the earth with precious gold
Celebration I fly
Your light lifts me higher
Freedom with even larger wings
Free to soar, to play, to fly higher

Scars still remain
Reminding of the painful process endured
But oh how beautiful
I reflect the Wind as I feel it close

You cut the string that holds the kite
It flies away
I fly away
Into the arms
That freed me to soar

-J.M.

Life Line

The sun signaled the glorious new day, and Desire and Victoria bounced out of their tent with such enthusiasm it was hard to contain. Everybody quickly packed up camp, probably faster than any other time before.

"This is going to be incredible!" Desire said to Joshua as the group was gathering.

"I've been waiting for this day all my life," he said, beaming with excitement as he gazed at the green land his ancestors spoke about years before.

"It's finally here!" Victoria joined in.

"This is it, let's go." Joshua led the way down the Last Mountain.

As they hiked, Desire saw a massive waterfall off in the distance that was sure to water the whole region. That must be what Joshua had tried to describe from his dreams so many months before.

The group made it to the base of the Last Mountain several hours later and proceeded to hike west towards the Pastures. From a distance, Desire noticed that Joshua, Victoria, and some of the others stopped in their tracks. She couldn't understand why they were just standing there when the Golden Pastures were so near. But when she got closer, she saw what hindered them. It was the very same thing that would hold her back from going into the land of her dreams. There, before them, stood a raging river.

The violent path of currents was the only thing separating them from the stunning Pastures, which Desire could now see so clearly just on the other side. Joshua explored the area but couldn't find an easy entry. They would have to cross the turbulent waters if they were to make it to the Golden Pastures.

Desire was so close yet so far once again.

Luckily, Victoria had spotted a fallen tree near the foot of the mountain. Joshua decided they could use it as a bridge to cross. It appeared to be the safest way to get to the other side, although safe would be an overstatement. Trying to swim across would be a sure way to drown. The undercurrents were likely to swallow up any daring soul and there were no calm waters in sight. One of the worst things about going over the dangerous rapids was that Desire would have to do it alone, with no hand-holding from her friends. No one else could cross this obstacle for her.

If she fell, she would be dragged into the waters and have to fend for her life.

Great, another dangerous and seemingly impossible risk to take.

After witnessing some close calls of others walking across then slipping and landing hard on the tree trunk, she decided her best strategy would be to straddle the thin log and slide across.

Her turn had come.

She scrambled onto the fallen tree and began to slowly inch across. The rough bark scraped her skin and her legs were soaked from the rowdy waters as she slid forward. She made it about halfway there.

She looked to her left at the waters and started to panic. Her heart accelerated. Her muscles tightened. She started to shiver and found it hard to catch her breath.

If she slipped, the violent river beneath her would sweep her away, and the only hope of a possible rescue would be a line of rope thrown out to her. But what if she couldn't reach it? She had never swum a day in her life. There were no streams or rivers in the Bronze Hills. The only water she remembered being there was that from the well, and she had no fond memories of that.

She was all alone.

There was only room for one person at a time to cross. The weight of any more was sure to snap the tree trunk. Desire was too far away for anyone to offer a hand.

With the water spraying in her face, she brushed her hair back. Amidst the sound of the moving waters, she heard faint voices of encouragement: "You've nearly made it! Take your time." She did take her time. Her arms continued to shake as she hugged the drenched log.

Focus, Desire, focus, you're almost there. You can do it. Her almost audible voice spurred her on. She looked across the river to the other side and saw her friends cheering her on. She saw the Pastures painted in the background.

She *could* do it. She knew she *needed* to do it. She had to see the fulfillment of the Legend, to experience the full life. After the exhausting journey, she had to make it across, not only for herself but for her mother, her father, and for everyone she left behind. Now was not the time to give up.

She took one deep breath and gathered every ounce of courage she could muster. Straddling the log, she used her arms to push herself up and move toward the other side. Inch by inch she slid until, almost there, a friend reached out his hand to help her step firmly onto the other side.

Still shivering, she sat on the river bank while she waited for the others to overcome the treacherous waters.

"Come on, Victoria! I know you can do it," Desire cheered. It was now her turn to encourage the others.

After making sure all the others had made it over safely, Joshua was the last person to cross the waters. When he stepped onto the bank on the side of the Golden Pastures, they all knew that the time, *their time*, had finally come. They gathered as a group and ran toward the land of their dreams.

Wide Awake

Joshua, Desire, and the others sprinted towards their true destiny. As they went, Desire noticed drastic changes taking place. She saw the faces of her fellow travelers become illuminated as they crossed over from the edges of the Silver Mountain region and into the Golden Pastures. She saw the earth beneath her feet change from dark shades of silver to light shades of gold. Running farther into an open field, she threw off her sandals and felt the bed of grass between her toes. When she jumped, she felt as if she was floating, as if she was being carried for moments by the gentle wind that filled the land.

Questions streamed through her head.

Is this really happening? Am I asleep and dreaming? What's this tingling feeling I have inside?

She could hardly believe that after all this time she had finally made it.

She saw that the Golden Pastures were dressed with a beautiful array of flowers, covered in a rainbow of colors. The land was filled with an abundance of luscious fruit trees. The grapes were ripe and plump and the oranges so juicy that it felt as if she was drinking a glass of fresh squeezed orange juice when taking a bite. Pomegranates, mangos, bananas, plums, and cherries were in endless supply. Cashew and pistachio nuts were readily available and vegetables of all kinds filled the land.

Desire was overwhelmed. This land was even better than the Legend had described. Deeper into the Pastures, the roaring river split off into veins of smaller and calmer streams of fresh water all around. There were several waterfalls scattered throughout the land as well. Butterflies fluttered along the flowers that decorated the stream banks and animals played in the fields. There were clear blue skies that day, and the land's beauty was magnified in the sunlight. The temperature was just right, warm with a fresh breeze.

Desire, along with the other Visionaries, danced boldly in the beauty of the new land. Victoria's countenance instantly changed in that place. She danced triumphantly without any hint of being weighed down by the reality of who her father was. Victoria told Desire that as soon as she stepped into the pastures, she felt that her ties to King Laird had been completely broken.

For Desire, the Pastures were more immense than she could have ever hoped or dreamed of. Joy exploded inside of her, more than she had experienced in the past. The struggles in the barren valleys and the challenges she faced climbing the mountains were nothing in comparison to what she was experiencing now. She was so blinded, in a good way, by the magnificence of the Golden Pastures that the Silver Mountains with everything in them quickly faded away in the shadow of their beauty. It was like a fairy tale come true for her. She felt as if her heart was bursting inside her. She felt more alive and free than she ever had before.

***

As the months went by, Desire and the thirty others established themselves in the Golden Pastures and built log cabins there. Desire's home overlooked the meadows and from the back of her house, she had a view of the Last Mountain. Trees surrounded her home and made it a haven of tranquility where she could hear birds singing throughout the morning hours. Her Aunt Clemente lived with her there. The journey had softened her aunt's disposition, and with Desire's mother gone and her father still settled in the Bronze Hills, she appreciated having some family close by. Victoria shared a home with a few of the others, and Joshua had his home just down the stream from Desire's.

***

About a year after they first entered the Pastures, Joshua sat outside his home and reminisced with Desire one spring afternoon.

"You know, as I've watched you, you've become like the trees I see in this place. Your life has blossomed by following the Legend to the very end. You bring nourishment and strength to others just by being you."

For the first time in a while, it was Desire who was speechless and a woman of few words. She was never good at taking compliments, and she wasn't quite sure how to respond to Joshua's poetic attempts. She felt her cheeks turn red.

"Hey, look at that bird," she said, pointing off into the distance, "Did you see its colors?"

***

Desire and the Visionaries continued to welcome their new life. They went fishing, hiking, and some of them even went rock climbing for enjoyment! Desire learned how to paint and used the juices from the berries for her paints, thick blades of grass for her brushes, and dried out banana leaves for her canvases. She even learned how to swim in the pool that formed at the bottom of one of the waterfalls. Her days were filled with joy, thankfulness, and a deep contentment that she had never experienced before. The land even lavished upon them a great return for their farming efforts. When they grew and harvested the crops, they received a hundred fold of whatever they sowed in the ground. No other region could compare with the abundance found in the Golden Pastures.

But Desire still felt that there was something missing.

While she had everything she needed in that place and more, she couldn't fully let go of Sam, Kaden, Dawn, and her father. They weren't there with her, and she felt their absence.

Desire grieved that Kaden chose to stop the momentum that would have catapulted her into making her dream become a reality. Kaden was *so* close to letting the fullness of life capture her, but instead she sabotaged her chance and said she wouldn't be able to handle it. Desire just knew that it must weigh heavily on Kaden to see the Pastures from that mountaintop every day.

Desire had a growing sense that there was still even more awaiting her and the Visionaries if they continued to journey on. She tried to imagine what could be better than life in the Golden Pastures. She wondered if anything could top their land. But she soon began to wonder if she and the other Visionaries needed to embark on a new journey, not to a foreign land of hope like before, but back into the dry, colorless, and muted terrain they had come from.

She questioned if it was good enough to take hold of the promise of the Legend just for herself. She wondered if she must also share it with others. She sensed from talking with Dawn, Sam, and Kaden in the past that they shared the same dream, that they truly believed the Legend. Desire felt that they were destined for this place too, they had just been sidetracked, that's all.

Even though Desire had failed to convince the others to move forward, she anticipated it would be different this time if she went back. She was now living proof that the promise of the Legend existed. They would *have* to listen to and believe her this time.

Not too long after this revelation had come to her, she sought out Joshua outside his home.

"Joshua, I need to talk to you." She interrupted him from chopping wood.

"Of course." He left what he was doing and led her to a bench where they both sat down.

"What is it?"

"Do you ever think about the others; your sister and the Dreamers, Sam and the Secured, Dawn and the Liberated?" she asked.

"They've actually been on my mind a lot lately. Why do you ask?"

"Well, I've been thinking..."

True Colors Fly

"Every evening as I sit on my porch, I stare at the Last Mountain, wondering, hoping, and longing to see some of the others come down to join us here." Desire continued on, "Sometimes in the middle of the night I wake up thinking I hear Kaden's voice, and I look out of the window to see if she's coming to meet us..."

"Lately, I've had this idea, it's been consuming me. You know it's been over a year now that we've been here. Well, what if maybe it's time we stopped waiting for them to come to us? What if instead of us hoping and praying for them to come, we thought about going back to encourage them to return and live here with us?"

Joshua's eyes met hers, he was about to say something but Desire continued.

"You know, I'd love to see Kaden and see how she's doing, to have the chance to see if she's at a place now where she would want to join us. Even Sam, although I know we're in two different places now, but I still would like to see him and the Secured, tell them how breathtaking this place really is, that it really does exist, and that it's even more amazing than what the Legend says about it."

Desire began to understand at an even deeper level the great tragedy it was when those close to her chose to settle for silver rather than gold; when they were content to settle for less than what was freely available. She continued believing out loud, "I would love to see my dad again if that's at all possible."

"You know what Desire?" Joshua said. "I think you're on to something. We'll have to plan carefully though if we want to go back into the Bronze Hills, we still don't know how hostile the area is or if it's even safe to return there at all. When we get that far, we'll have to send out some spies to scope the Bronze Hills before we can re-enter it. You also need to realize that after all this time, the promise of the Legend might have faded for some of them. Our friends might already be so settled in their new lands that what once drew them to this place has now died inside of them. It's important you—"

"I know that, but even if that is the case, I think we can be the sparks to rekindle what was once there in their hearts," Desire was sure of herself.

Joshua smiled. "Well, we should waste no time gathering the others to plan another journey to go back, at least as far as Freedom Mountain at this point," he said. At his ready and strategic response, Desire wondered if this was something that had been stirring inside of him for some time as well.

***

Desire, Joshua, Victoria, and about fifteen others agreed to set out on the new adventure. The Golden Pastures would become the base from which their journey would begin all over again. In the process, these Visionaries would move even farther down the path of becoming True Revolutionaries.

They made plans to return to convince each group. They would go to Kaden and the Dreamers first, then Sam and the Secured, Dawn and the Liberated, and hopefully have the chance to find Desire's father and the others who were still back in the Bronze Hills. They had a divine mission, a new dream to follow, a new Legend to create. They also had a commitment to see it through. *This* was their destiny.

Desire didn't know how it would end, if anyone would return with them to the Pastures. Regardless, she was determined to go back to help the others see that there was so much more awaiting them than the limited freedom they had settled for. She desperately wanted to help her friends move from a life of dangerous comfort and incomplete freedom to a life full of adventure and abundance.

Thriving at last and continuing to follow her heart, she was ready to return.

This was no mistake, it *was* the right decision, and she felt it so strongly. She also knew it could cost her dearly. Nevertheless, she prepared to journey on...

After Words

I sincerely hope that you have been stirred once again to take those risky steps towards fulfilling the dreams inside your heart. Today is the only day we have to move towards our dreams. It's time to break out of our stagnant circumstances and take chances once again. Many obstacles and setbacks *will* come our way as we journey out of our comfort zones. Not everyone will stay on our same path or understand us as we follow our hearts. Nevertheless, I highly encourage each and every one of you not to settle for silver when your destiny is gold. You may become disillusioned at times as you walk on this path, but at least you will never have any regrets.

While we don't have to live anyone else's dream, we do have a responsibility to live our own. Each of us has a dream inside of us. Some of us have more than one. A difference can be made in the lives of others when we step out and fulfill our specific, and I believe God-given dreams. Beauty comes as a result when we follow our hearts. Others are blessed, challenged, and empowered when we take hold of our lives and make decisions towards living our passions, towards following our deepest desires. There are people around us who are waiting for us to come alive, people who need for us to live our dreams so that their lives will be better. It was Martin Luther King Jr. who once said, "I have a dream," and look what happened when he followed his heart. It's time for us to do the same.

So now, because other lives depend on it, including your own, may the True Revolutionaries please step forward and march towards your destinies.

Music

U2's song "Bad" connects well with the heart of the overall story. Some other songs I feel share a similar thread to the story in one way or another, presented in order of appearance as they relate to the themes in the story, are:

"Dare You to Move" by Switchfoot
"Glósóli" by Sigur Rós (the music video)
"Finally Free" by Nichole Nordeman
"Painting Pictures of Egypt" by Sarah Groves
"Umbrellas" by Sleeping At Last
"Fair" by Remy Zero
"Goodbye" by Plankeye
"Unless You Cry" by Bekah Driscoll
"Walk On" by U2
"Where the Streets Have No Name" by U2 (the music video, live in Boston 2001)

Media

I invite you to continue your journey with Silver to Gold by going to the book's website:

www.silvertogold.com

Here you will find:
-Questions for reflection
-Group study questions
-A test to see which character you are most like
-More about the story behind the story
-Link to the author's personal blog and contact information
-Opportunity to share your thoughts on the book and/or testimonials
-Various other extras

The Story Behind the Story

I want to share with you some of the story behind the *Silver to Gold* story. Before I begin writing about some developments and the process of the "silver to gold" philosophy being formed in me, here's a little background. I grew up in Anaheim, California, and spent way too much time on the 55 freeway. One of the reasons for this was because that was the route I had to take to get to my local surf spot. I spent a good portion of the early mornings of my teenage years and even twenties at the beach bodyboarding. To get out of the gridlock and the crowds, I loved to travel to new places to find good waves. During my college days, I once traveled to Costa Rica by myself in search of surf and to see the beauty there.

Less than a month after I graduated from a university in California in 2000, at twenty-two years old, I moved to Mozambique for six months to serve the poor. This was just after the floods devastated the country. My time there was life-changing to say the least. While living at the orphanage as my base, I had the opportunity to help teenage prostitutes get off of the streets, feed the poor, and care for orphans. I was also a part of organizing several medical clinics in the refuge camps as well as helping to plant a church. The joy I saw in their lives there even when they had so little was profoundly beautiful.

I moved back to California at the end of that year and prepared to go back to Africa to serve the poor. Because of various circumstances, I ended up staying in California where I designed, developed, and implemented an intensive five week discipleship course with about fifteen youth from my church. This turned out to have a great impact on many of them, and was a great privilege for me to be a part of.

Throughout the next couple of years, a story had been forming in my heart that I believed would encourage people to pursue their dreams, to not settle for silver when they are meant for gold. I zealously printed 2,000 copies of this little story, formerly known as *From Silver to Gold: An Adventure from Freedom to Abundance*, and passed them out for free at a rally in San Francisco in 2003. I didn't realize at that time that there was more of the story to be formed. At that point, the story had no dialogue and no characters; it was a rough sketch of what was later to come.

Throughout the next few years, I ended up transitioning into a career with Starbucks coffee. I grew in the company and enjoyed it very much while continuing to develop my little story. I also took several writing classes off and on and attended a few writing conferences. All this was for the purpose of shaping my story. As I continued with my career, I always felt there was something else I was supposed to be doing after my time there. I knew deep

From Silver to Gold

An Adventure from Freedom to Abundance

by
Jen Miskov

down I was meant to be involved in teaching, training, speaking, or coaching, and developing young leaders, whatever that might look like. I also had this growing desire to study in England and I knew that if I wanted to teach one day, I would need a Ph.D. The one thing that always held me back from pursuing more education was the money issue. It had already taken me several years to pay off my loans from my undergraduate studies, even after I had already worked multiple jobs while in school, and I was not looking forward to being in debt again. Because of this, I put off returning to school...for six more years!

A few years ago, one of the girls from the discipleship group I mentioned earlier said the following to me one night: "Don't settle for silver when God wants to give you gold." Those words were powerful and struck me at a deep level. Maybe it was because I was in a situation where I needed to let go of something that was holding me back from more in my life, or maybe it was the fact that she had spoken my own words directly back to me. What she said had been my line for years. I had challenged so many people to not settle for less than God's best in their lives and to hear those words again made them come alive even more.

As *Silver to Gold* continued to form in and through me over the years, sometimes I would move forward to try and get it published, only to get rejection letter after rejection letter. Nevertheless, I continued working on it. I realized, though, that since the heart of the story is an encouragement for others to live their dreams, I must be living mine if there is to be any integrity in the story. If I am not living my dreams, if I am settling for silver in areas of my life when I'm meant for gold, then who is going to listen to me, who is going to believe in the story? So as a result of trying to stay true to the heart of the story, in 2007, I quit my job, sold my car, said goodbye to all my friends and family, and let go of my comfortable life in California to go on an unknown adventure to England.

Now that I am in England, I am enjoying pursuing a Ph.D. I admit that the transition I faced the first year away from home wasn't easy. But after some time, I have felt more connected and have had some opportunities here that I never would have had back in the OC. Besides meeting some great people here, in the summer of 2008, I got to be a part of leading a team of students to put on a week of fun events to welcome new international students to my university. I also ran my first ever half-marathon. Currently, I help lead a group through my church that does free healing prayer right in the heart of the city center.

I really do believe that there is something beautiful, maybe even supernatural, in taking risks, in following one's heart, in pursuing one's dreams. Whatever your dream may be, even if it seems like it is taking forever, I encourage you to not give up. If you stay on its path and keep moving towards it, eventually you'll get there, some quicker than others. One of my dreams took seven years and a lot of hard work, sacrifice, risk, and support from others, but I'm so glad the time has finally arrived. And I know that if you don't give up, your time will soon come too. Well, that's all I have to say for now. If this book has made a difference or impacted your life in any way, I would love to hear your story. Feel free to contact me through the book's website where I will be posting testimonials and personal life stories. Thanks for coming on this little journey with me. I hope you have enjoyed the adventure.

Acknowledgements

So many people throughout the past seven years have helped me on this project that there is not enough room to thank each one personally, but to all of you who were a part of this in one way or another, know that you have left a stamp on this book and in my heart, and I am very grateful for your support.

Special thanks to my parents, Joe and Dee, who have always supported me and have never given up on me, who loved the story even when it was unfinished. Thanks to my brother Joe (the fourth, to be precise), who helped me greatly with the final edits all while working full time in Sudan. He is not only the greatest brother in the world but also one of my best friends. To my sister Darla, who has always believed in me and who has a tremendous amount of grace, and to my amazing nephew Justin who is growing up too quickly but who has such a precious heart. They, along with my close friends, have stood by me and encouraged me all along the way.

Noted here are only a few of the names of those who have helped me over the years on this story in one way or another: Cathy Morrill helped with the first draft in 2003, Bonnie Hanson helped off and on for the last several years. Alice S. Bass provided a crucial manuscript evaluation when my book was nearing publication. Jo Stagg, Andrew Pain, and my brother Joe have acted almost as midwives (sorry, Joe and Andrew, I know you're boys) in helping me in the final stages. Without their commitment to me and support in editing, I'm not sure how many more years this story would have taken to make it to the general public. Thanks to Chris Lauer for envisioning the artwork some years ago and Ruthie Gallo, not only for being a great friend and an incredible support to me personally, but also for her creativity in cover design ideas. Special thanks for Ollie, Oliver, and Kellé at IE Design for their support in this project as well as finalizing the book cover. I want to thank Joanna Hield for taking my headshot, Yadira Perez for her long-term support in my life and for proof-reading the final draft, and Affi Luc Agbodo for his support with marketing.

I am grateful for people like Bob and Penny Fulton who have been influential in my own journey and who have spent much time in the Golden Pastures themselves. I would like to give a "shout out" to some I used to like to call "my girls" over the years who are now no longer girls but beautiful women. They have become great friends and inspirations to me. I also want to thank my friends both new and old, near and far. Friends who have stayed committed to me over the years and those who have quit their jobs to travel to foreign lands always touch my heart in one way or another.

Lastly, I am indebted and inspired by others who have gone before me who have pursued their dreams and have lived or are currently living their lives loudly: Joan of Arc, Martin Luther King Jr., Heidi Baker, Bono, Carrie Judd Montgomery, Saint Francis of Assisi, and Jesus, the truest love revolutionary of them all. Most of all, I am thankful to God for putting this story in my heart and guiding me all along the way through the Silver Mountains and into His Golden Pastures for my life. It's been such an exciting journey!

Impact

By buying this book you have made a great impact and have helped many different people follow their dreams. A percentage of the author's profits will go directly towards helping the people in Mozambique to have a better life so that they will have the opportunity to pursue their dreams one day. Another percentage of the profits will be used to support people who are actively pursuing their dreams. Most of the additional profit will go directly toward helping the author pay for one of her own dreams of studying in England. So please know that in the process of buying the book, you have touched lives and have become a believer that dreams can come true.

The Silver to Gold Project

If you have been encouraged through this story and want to share its message, here are some practical ways that you can help.

Share how the story has impacted you with those around you. What thoughts has it raised or how has it encouraged you? This could be informally over lunch with co-workers, a planned coffee date, or even through your local book club.

If you are a part of a book club, suggest having them go through *Silver to Gold* together. You can utilize the study group questions found on the website to support you in facilitating deeper discussion.

Give this book away as a gift. It can even be used as a coffee table or bathroom book. It's ideal for graduating students as well as others who are undergoing a transition.

Support anyone you know who has been brave enough to enter into a Master's or Ph.D program. This book can encourage them to make it to the end.

Help to promote this book through Facebook, MySpace and other social networks by joining the book's Facebook group, adding the fan page, and subscribing to the blog. Invite friends whom you think might connect with the story to join the book's group and fan page as well.

Add a link to the book's website (www.silvertogold.com) to your website or blog and encourage others to check it out.

Write a review for your local newspaper, magazine, blog, or website. Have discussions of this book on different forums. Write book reviews on amazon.com and other sites. Send the author a testimonial or personal life story of how this book has impacted you.

Help spread this book internationally by sending it to friends abroad.

If you own a business, consider linking this book to your company by offering to sell copies through your business. Discount rates on books for re-sale can be arranged so that you will be able to make money and build your business as well as support this project.

Leadership Training: Consider using this book as an alternative and exciting new way to develop your employees or your team. This book can support you as you lead an organization toward a specific vision and goal. It can be used to build morale and bring encouragement in the workplace in the midst of recession and potential crisis.

You may want to invite the author to come and speak with your organization on some of the themes found in the book. You can contact her through the book's website.

Help get this message into schools by giving a copy to teachers.

Ask your local bookstore to stock this book.

Buy extra copies of the book and give to organizations you support or to individuals you believe in and want to see succeed even more.

If you have a newsletter through your church or any other organization you are a part of, find out if you can highlight or do a book review in the newsletter.

Rather than focusing on marketing the book, focus on genuinely sharing with others how it has affected you. Without giving away the whole story, share how the themes can translate into real life.

There are many more creative ways to share this message so feel free to be inspired and creative in how you go about it. If you have additional ideas, the author would be interested to hear what you are doing. You can contact her through the book's website at **www.silvertogold.com**.

SilvertoGold

May the following question haunt you every step in your journey: journey:

"Why settle for silver when you're meant for Gold?"

5759052R0

Made in the USA
Charleston, SC
30 July 2010